THE
D-WORD

THE D-WORD

DIVORCE THROUGH A CHILD'S EYES

TARA EISENHARD

iUniverse, Inc.
Bloomington

The D-Word
Divorce Through a Child's Eyes

iUniverse books may be ordered through booksellers or by contacting:

iUniverse
1663 Liberty Drive
Bloomington, IN 47403
www.iuniverse.com
1-800-Authors (1-800-288-4677)

Because of the dynamic nature of the Internet, any web addresses or links contained in this book may have changed since publication and may no longer be valid. The views expressed in this work are solely those of the author and do not necessarily reflect the views of the publisher, and the publisher hereby disclaims any responsibility for them.

ISBN: 978-1-4759-3139-6 (sc)
ISBN: 978-1-4759-3141-9 (e)
ISBN: 978-1-4759-3140-2 (dj)

Library of Congress Control Number: 2012910093

Printed in the United States of America

iUniverse rev. date: 8/10/2012

For you.
Yes, *you.*

Preface

always wanted to write for the young-adult crowd. When I began this work, I thought that's what I was doing. I was wrong. A few pages into it I realized that I wasn't writing this piece for "Gina." I was writing it for her parents, grandparents, teachers and a multitude of other adults who might influence her during such an impressionable time.

For many years, I've held onto the passionate belief that families should evolve and not dissolve through the process of a divorce. For just as many years, I've been saddened by the frequency with which the opposite effect comes to fruition. My intention for this book is to allow those involved in a divorce to regard the situation from different perspectives. My hope is that such consideration will promote more positive interactions, thus encouraging a healthier transition for divorcing families.

I'd like to recognize my parents, for showing me that a good divorce is possible. I'd also like to express gratitude to my ex-husband for helping me attain my own good divorce. To those of you who served, and will serve, as teachers throughout my quest for knowledge, thank you.

All interactions provide an opportunity to learn and grow.

Reader, I wish you a peaceful and prosperous evolution...

Chapter 1: June

It was five days before my twelfth birthday when it happened, when my whole life changed. It was a Wednesday night in June, just a couple weeks before the end of the school year.

My mom went shopping after dinner, leaving my dad home with me and my brother, Danny. We cleaned up the kitchen together and then set to work on the rest of the house. We had a pillow fight in the living room, and we played catch with a plastic orange from the dining room table. My dad always found a way to make chores seem like fun. Even when he helped us with our homework, he pretended that he was the student and Danny and I were the teachers. He asked us to teach him the lesson, and by the time we were done, we didn't need his help at all!

I was upset when my mom came home and my parents started fighting. It was past bedtime, and I was supposed to be asleep, but they woke me up. It wasn't unusual. The fight was pretty standard: they were arguing about my dad not sweeping behind the toilet and my mom being a drill sergeant and my grandmother being too nosey and my aunt being a showoff ... And then he said it. Actually, he didn't say anything at first. It was oddly quiet for a moment, and then he said, "Jill, I don't want to live like this anymore. It's not fair to the kids, and it's not fair to us. I think we should get a divorce."

My mother started shouting again, but I didn't hear what she was saying because Danny burst into my room. He was crying as he jumped on my bed and clung to me. I put my arms around him and rubbed his back.

"Gina, I'm scared. What's going to happen now?" he asked me.

I didn't know what to tell him. I didn't know *what* was going to happen. The truth was that I was as scared and confused as he was, but I wasn't crying. I didn't cry because I had to be strong for Danny. He was only six years old.

"Don't worry," I told him. "It's going to be OK. They're just fighting like usual. You know how they say things they don't mean."

The yelling stopped then because my older brother, Kevin, came home. Kevin was a senior in high school and he worked evenings at a pizza shop downtown. Normally I was jealous of the fact that Kevin got to stay out so late on school nights, but that night I was glad he came home when he did. Danny went back to his room. Mom and Dad gave it a rest, and I was finally able to get some sleep.

The next morning everyone acted normal. After school, during dinner and after dinner, there was no fighting. No mention of the D-word. I was relieved! I thought maybe it had all been a bad dream. In fact, Mom and Dad actually seemed to get along pretty well over the next couple weeks.

***

My birthday came and went. The last day of school came and went. The weekend after school ended, Dad took me to his parents' house. My grandmother's birthday is the day before mine, and my cousin Laurie's birthday is three days later. She's a year younger than me, and Grandma said that this year she thought we were old enough to go on a cruise to celebrate. I'd found out about it in December and had been looking forward to the trip for months.

We were halfway to their house when Dad turned down the radio and told me the news.

"Gina, we need to talk," he said.

And then I *knew*. I knew that the D-word hadn't been a dream. I knew it was real, and it was all coming true. My throat was dry, and my eyes were wet. I turned and looked out the window. There were horses in a pasture by the side of the road.

"Gina? Can you look at me?"

I shook my head.

"Well, OK…" he began. "There's no easy way to say this. Your mom and I have decided … Well, I'm … I'm going to be moving. I found an apartment downtown, and I'm going to move while you're on your cruise next week."

I choked back the tears. How could they do this to me? At the beginning of the summer! The beginning of my vacation! How could Dad leave when I wouldn't be there to say goodbye? And why didn't he ask me if I wanted to go with him?

"Do you have any questions?" he asked after I'd been silent for some time.

I shook my head again. I still wouldn't look at him. I stared at the cornfields outside the window. I didn't know if I wanted to cry or if I wanted to scream. And I felt empty too, like there was a big hole in me. Right in the center of my chest, or maybe my stomach. I couldn't be sure because on top of everything else, I also felt numb.

Dad started talking again. I guess he didn't like the fact that I didn't have anything to say. "I want you to know that this has nothing to do with you," he said.

Yeah, right, I thought. *It has everything to do with me. It's my life. My parents. My family!*

"Your mom and I love you very much," Dad kept talking. "It's not your fault, and we're not mad at you. So if you have any questions about anything, you can talk to us. We've been working together on our plans, and we're trying hard to do what's best for you kids."

Not my fault? *Of course it's not my fault!* Why did he think I would think this was because of me? I wasn't the one screaming in the kitchen late at night. I wasn't the one who got mad about the electric bill or the credit cards or whatever else they fought about. No way … this wasn't my fault. It was *theirs!*

"And I know this might seem odd to say, but I'm doing this for you. I want you and your brothers to be happy and relaxed at home. You shouldn't have to hear me and your mom fighting. I want you to have a better life."

A better life? Was he crazy? I couldn't imagine how things could be any better without my dad around. When the view out the window turned to hotels and warehouses, I wiped my eyes, looked at Dad and asked, "What about Danny? Is he going with you?"

"No," Dad looked relieved. He must've been happy that I finally said something. "Your mom feels very strongly that both you and Danny should stay in the house with her. That's your home, and there's no reason for you to move. Your mom and I decided you will both stay with me every other weekend. But we can still talk on the phone and email. I'll send you some pictures of my apartment as soon as I get settled."

"Are you still going to see Kevin?" I asked. My dad wasn't Kevin's father, but Kevin didn't see his real dad, so he and Dad had always been close.

"I'm not sure," Dad admitted. "I'll discuss that with Kevin. Obviously I love him very much, but he's an adult, and he's going off to college in the fall ... we'll just have to see how things go."

I turned the radio up again and turned back toward the window. *What a great way to start my vacation,* I thought with a sigh.

***

When we got to Grandma and Grandpa's house, they didn't say anything about the D-word, but Grandpa looked very serious. He and Grandma spent extra time hugging and then waited for me to run off with Laurie so they could talk to my dad. I wondered if they were mad at him.

Laurie and I escaped to our old tree house where we used to have tea parties. We hadn't done that in a long time. Instead, Laurie had stocked it with magazines and nail polish. I chose a bottle of dark blue. The color was almost black, and it matched my mood.

I didn't say anything about my parents, but I could tell that Laurie knew. Eventually, she looked up from her pink toes and said, "Gina, I am so sorry."

I didn't know what to say. It was all so new to me. And it bothered me that Laurie found out either before or at the same time that I did. Still, it was nice to hear something so simple. I thanked her, and she told me she couldn't imagine how I must feel.

"It's weird," I said. "You see it happen to other people, and you always think it won't happen to you."

Laurie nodded, shook her bottle of polish, and began a second coat on her toes. I was glad because I didn't want to talk about it anymore. I felt a little better, and I hoped my situation wouldn't ruin our vacation.

***

Our ship was huge. It was big enough to get lost on, but I couldn't lose the feeling in the pit of my stomach. Everywhere I turned, I saw moms and dads swimming, painting, eating, or shopping with their kids. I thought about the vacations I'd been on with my parents and I realized that we'd never take another trip together. I felt sad and alone.

I couldn't stop thinking about what was going to happen when I got home. I wondered if my dad would be there to greet me before going back to his apartment. I wondered if my mom would be in a better mood without him around. I couldn't imagine what my dad was going to take from the house. I had no idea what it would look like when I returned. I dreaded telling my friends.

There were times when I started crying for no reason. I'd be having a great time and then I'd remember the D-word and my eyes would fill up with tears. One night we went to a show in the main theater. I was smiling and laughing until I saw a man walk up the aisle, carrying a little boy who was sleeping. I remembered my dad carrying me and Danny to bed when we fell asleep early. I held my breath in hopes that it would stop the tears, but it didn't work. My eyes watered and my nose ran. I sniffled once, as quietly as possible. Grandma heard me anyway. She reached for my hand and gave it a warm squeeze.

"I don't like this number either," she whispered. Then she winked and nodded toward the stage. "But keep watching. They'll sing a new song soon enough."

Chapter 2: July

Grandma and Grandpa drove me home the day after the cruise was over. I was nervous about going back to the house where my dad no longer lived. I could tell they were nervous too. Instead of trying to make conversation in the car, I opened a book and started reading. When I felt sick from staring at the words, I leaned my head against the window and went to sleep.

We pulled into the driveway four hours after leaving my grandparents' house. I got out and stretched while Grandpa retrieved my luggage from the trunk. Grandma and Grandpa each took a bag and helped me carry them inside.

My mom met us in the doorway. She gave me a big hug and told me that she had really, really missed me and she didn't know what she'd do without me for another day. Then she straightened up and turned to my grandparents.

Her smile disappeared and she said sharply, "I didn't expect you'd be coming in."

"Well, we couldn't leave Gina on the curb with all these bags," Grandpa told her with a chuckle.

"And," Grandma began, "We wanted to offer …. We're heading over to visit Doug and see his new apartment. If you'd like, we can take the kids—"

"Oh, no," my mother interrupted with a nervous laugh. "I don't think that's a very good idea. Do you? The place isn't fully furnished yet! It's hardly appropriate to take the kids there."

I wanted to tell her that it's not appropriate for my dad to have to live somewhere else just so he could get away from her! But I didn't say anything. Instead, I grabbed my bags and headed to my room.

The house seemed different. It was quieter, and there were things missing. It didn't look empty, but there were little holes that made it feel incomplete. It made *me* feel incomplete too. Some pictures were gone from the walls, like the one of my dad with the big fish he caught in a contest the previous summer. There were books missing from the shelves. And his overstuffed recliner wasn't in the living room anymore. I held my breath so I wouldn't cry as I hurried down the hall to my bedroom and shut the door.

I dropped my bags, took a deep breath, and closed my eyes. When I opened them again, I looked around my room, hoping to find comfort in familiar things. And that's when I saw a stuffed bunny and the envelope with my name on it. I sat down on my bed and opened the letter.

Gina,

I know you want a pet bunny, but you're aware of how your mom feels about that. So this is the best I can do. Maybe someday when I buy a house I can get you the real thing. Until then, please take care of this guy. I've been calling him 'Henry.' I told him how much I love you and I asked him to keep you company.

I'm sorry this is hard. I wish it didn't have to be, but I think this is the only way to make things better for all of us. I promise that it won't always be so difficult and confusing. I won't be too far away and I'll see you next weekend. I love you. I miss you. I'll see you soon.

Love,
Dad

When I slid the envelope under my pillow, my hand found the little book of jokes he'd left for me. It was a nice thought, but I didn't feel like laughing. I looked out the window and saw Danny in the yard. He was sitting at the edge of his sandbox, and he had something in his hands. I decided to go check on him.

When I got outside, I could see that he was playing with the kind of puzzle where you have to shift the pieces around to make a picture. I asked him if he'd seen Grandma and Grandpa.

"That's where I got this," he told me.

"Oh," I said, sitting down next to him. "Have you seen Dad?"

Danny shook his head. "I wasn't here when he left. Mommy sent me to play at Peter's house. When I came back, Daddy was gone." He looked down at the ground and pointed to a remote-control car on the walkway. "He left that for me."

I wasn't in the mood to play, but I thought a distraction might be a good idea for Danny. I forced a smile and asked, "Would you like to play with your car now?"

"OK," he agreed, his face brightening a little.

***

The next day we had a cookout for the Fourth of July. My Aunt Tamara and cousins, Caleb and Ethan, came over. Mom said I could invite some friends too, so I called Jenny and Sarah, and they joined us. Kevin had to work that day, but he brought a couple pizzas home in the afternoon.

We ate a red, white and blue cake, ran through the sprinklers, and played various games. There were a few moments when I was having a great time and almost felt normal. Most of the time, I missed my dad. I kept expecting to see him cooking hamburgers on the grill or preparing a big fireworks display. I wondered how he was spending the weekend. At the same time, I was happy because I knew that when the guests went home, I wouldn't have to listen to my parents argue. They usually had their worst fights after big group get-togethers. Immediately, I felt guilty for being glad that he wasn't there.

After a few hours, Sarah asked where my dad was. I hadn't told anyone what was going on because I didn't know how to say it. Was I supposed to send a mass text message to everyone I knew? I asked my mom if Sarah, Jenny and I could take a walk, and she said it was OK as long as we came back in an hour. When we got away from the party, I just blurted it out.

"My parents are getting a divorce," I told them.

Jenny sighed. "Is that it? I was afraid your dad was hurt or sick!" Jenny's mom and dad got divorced when she was two years old. It was all she'd ever known, so she didn't think it was a big deal to have separated parents. And she didn't understand why people thought it was such a bad thing.

Sarah glared at Jenny and then turned to me. "Where did your dad go?" she asked. "And when are you going to see him?"

I told them the whole plan … about my dad getting an apartment downtown and how I was supposed to see him the next weekend and every other weekend after that. I told them how mad I was that nobody asked me what I wanted and who I wanted to live with. I told them that I felt like there was a big sign on me that said "divorced kid," and everyone who knew the situation was looking at me differently.

"How's your mom?" Jenny asked.

"Fine, I guess," I answered. "I haven't been here very much because of the cruise. She seems happy, but I think she's faking it. I've only been home since yesterday, but I think she's had about eight phone calls with my Aunt Tamara since then. And she used to complain a lot about Aunt Tamara. Now they're like, best friends. I don't get it."

Sarah wanted to help. "Do you need anything? Do you want to come to my house for a few days?"

"No, but thanks," I told her. "I've been away for a week. I really want to sleep in my own bed and see how things go around here."

Sarah gave me a hug. "Let me know if there is anything I can do for you, OK?" she said. "You don't have to go through this alone."

"Thanks," I told her. It was all I could say.

***

In the middle of the week, I got an email from my dad. It felt strange to get an email from someone I used to see every day. He told me that he missed me and he couldn't wait to hear all about the cruise. He said that he would have sent me something sooner, but he wanted to give me some space to get used to things, and he didn't want to add to my confusion. I liked that he was honest. He also sent me pictures of his apartment. It looked small and empty. He told me it's near the river, and there's a nice walking trail and an ice cream shop around the corner. He said he couldn't wait to see me on Friday night.

I didn't know what to say when I wrote back. My entire life had changed since the last time I saw him. I decided to keep it short:

Hi,

I miss you too. Your apartment looks nice. See you Friday!

I didn't know if I was supposed to tell Mom about the email. I felt like I should tell her, yet I also felt like I shouldn't tell her because I didn't want her to get mad. She didn't want me to go see my dad with my grandparents, so she might be really upset that he wrote to me.

During dinner that night, Mom asked about my day. Since she asked, I decided to tell her about the email from Dad. Immediately, I wished I hadn't said anything.

"Oh?" She seemed curious at first. "Pictures of the apartment, huh? How does it look?"

"Kinda empty right now," I said. "I guess he's just starting out, so there isn't much there."

"I see," Mom said, standing up from the table. "I'm finished eating. Please put your dishes in the sink when you're done."

She went into the kitchen and picked up the phone, then she went outside to the back patio. I guess she thought we wouldn't be able to hear her out there, but the windows were open and we heard everything. She called my dad to talk about the "condition" of his apartment.

"Sleeping bags on the floor?" she sounded like she didn't believe what he'd said.

"No, Doug. Absolutely not! You owe it to your children to provide them with acceptable bedding and the accommodations of a real home. They won't be staying with you until you can give them that. I don't think it's too much to ask, do you? After all they've been through!"

Dad must've suggested that he come to the house to visit because then she really got angry.

"How could you even *think* such a thing?! No! This is *my* house where I live with my children, and you have no business being here since you abandoned us! No."

I looked at Danny. He was pretending not to hear her as he nibbled his dinner roll and finished his grape juice. But I could tell he was listening because he was being very careful not to make any noise while he ate and drank.

So much for things being better, I thought. I learned quickly not to tell Mom when Dad sent me emails.

An hour later, Mom came back in the house. I could tell by her face that she'd been crying. She washed the dishes that were in the sink and then came to the family room where Danny was playing video games and I was on the computer.

"Kids, there's been a change of plans," she told us. "Your dad isn't ready for you to visit this weekend, so we're going to go camping with Aunt Tamara."

"And Caleb and Ethan?" Danny asked.

"No," Mom said. "It's their weekend with their dad."

I wondered why we couldn't sleep in sleeping bags at Dad's apartment, but it was OK to sleep in sleeping bags in a tent. After everything Mom had said about having a nice place to stay, it didn't make any sense. Nothing seemed to make sense anymore.

***

Two weeks went by, and it was almost time to go to my dad's apartment again. I had received a couple more emails from him, but they were short and didn't contain any new information. I wondered if Dad blamed me for telling Mom about his lack of furniture and then getting our weekend canceled.

My mom was still talking to Aunt Tamara a lot. It seemed they were bonding over the divorce. Aunt Tamara divorced my Uncle Ron about five years earlier, and she seemed to know everything. She was always telling my mom what to do. They talked about lawyers and bills and money. They also said a lot of mean things about my dad. They both seemed to hate him. I didn't like knowing they were talking about him that way. I remembered happy times as a family, and the way they talked made me wonder if everything I'd experienced in my life had been a lie.

Finally, it was time for Dad to pick us up for our visit. He pulled up to the curb outside and beeped his horn. I was surprised to see that he'd gotten a new car— a smaller one! When I sat inside, I realized that it didn't have leather seats like his old car did. And the floor mats were worn in places. It wasn't even a new car— he'd bought a used car!

Dad must've noticed my shock because when he leaned over to hug me, he whispered, "It's OK, Honey. I don't have a monthly payment anymore, and this car gets better gas mileage, so we can afford to take longer trips." I forced a smile and nodded my head.

Dad took us to dinner at one of those loud places with lots of bright lights and video games. Danny ordered chicken fingers, and I got a slice of pizza. We made small talk while we ate and as soon as Danny was finished with his chicken, he started jumping around and asking for quarters. Dad fished a dollar out of his pocket, and Danny sprinted to the change machine.

"So," Dad began. "How's it going?"

I was careful not to say anything about Mom because I didn't want to start any more problems between them.

"It's OK," I told him. "We've been spending a lot of time with Aunt Tamara. And sometimes I go to Sarah's house to swim in her pool in the evenings."

"So you're enjoying yourself? That's good." He seemed relieved. "Grandma and Grandpa told me that you and Laurie had a good time with them too."

"Yeah, the cruise was nice. And Laurie and I are the same size now, so we shared our clothes and didn't have to repeat outfits," I told him. I hadn't noticed it before, but I was tearing the crust of my pizza into little pieces. I suddenly realized how uncomfortable I felt.

Dad changed the subject. "Let's get back to my apartment," he said as he stood up. "I want you to see your room so you can start thinking about how you'd like to decorate it."

That sounded exciting. I called to Danny, and we headed to Dad's new home.

The apartment was on the second floor of an old building. We walked up the stairs and when he unlocked the door, he let me and Danny walk in first. We were standing in the living room. I saw Dad's Papa Bear Chair and the picture of him with the big fish. He also had some pictures of me and Danny when we were younger. I recognized them from my grandparents' house. Grandma must've given them to Dad because Mom kept all of our pictures. There was also an older couch in the living room, and a pile of folded blankets and a pillow were in the corner. Down the hall were two bedrooms and the bathroom. Danny's room was painted green, and it had beige carpet. There was a bed by the window and a dresser that I also recognized from Grandma and Grandpa's house. It was the dresser my dad used when he was younger.

My room was at the end of the hall. There were two big windows, and the walls were painted white. It had a closet and a full-length mirror. The bed was a full-sized mattress just sitting on the floor. The sheets were orange, and the bedspread was yellow, my favorite color. I knew my mom would be appalled that the bed had no box-spring or frame, but I thought it was kinda cool.

"I thought maybe tomorrow we could go shopping and you can pick out some posters to put in here," Dad said, putting his hand on my shoulder. "I want you to feel like this is another home for you. And your friends are welcome anytime."

"Thanks, Dad," I said.

That night we watched a movie in the living room. Dad didn't have cable, so we couldn't watch regular television. We made popcorn and stayed up until midnight. It was fun because we got to be together, and, thankfully, there wasn't any awkward conversation. By the time the movie was over, I felt pretty settled in my "second home."

***

Saturday we went shopping, and Jenny came along to pick out some items for my new room. I asked her to be there because she knew what it was like to have two bedrooms. It was a good thing because she was a big help.

"Picture frames are important," she coached me. "You'll want to have some pictures of your friends and family around at your dad's house. That is … as long as that's OK …?" She turned to my dad.

"Of course!" Dad answered. "I was actually going to suggest that Gina and Danny bring along pictures of their mother to put in their rooms."

I was relieved to hear that. Mom had been removing all the pictures of Dad from our house, and it made me sad. I knew which picture of my mom I wanted to bring. It was the one of me and Mom on a roller coaster at the local amusement park. In the picture, we were both screaming, and our hair was standing straight up. My mom hated that picture, but it reminded me of a fun day.

Jenny also helped me pick out some posters and other necessities. She suggested that I pack my outfits for each visit so I'd never be missing clothes that I wanted to wear to school. However, she said I should keep some things in both places. That way, I wouldn't have to pack them all the time. We shopped for an extra robe, nightshirt, hoodie with a zipper, sweatpants, underwear, slippers and socks.

When we were done selecting clothing, Jenny told me that I should also keep extra beauty products at my dad's. We grabbed some bottles of shampoo, conditioner and cream to wash my face.

Danny wanted to keep a separate wardrobe with Dad, so he picked out lots of clothes. It took a long time to ring up all of our purchases at the register, and I gasped when I saw the bill. I felt guilty because Dad had to get a smaller car, he didn't have cable, and we had just cost him several hundred dollars. When we got in the car, I apologized in addition to thanking him for everything.

Dad just grinned. "Think of it as a partial gift from your grandparents," he said. "We all want to be sure you have everything you need."

***

The rest of the weekend was fun. After shopping on Saturday, Jenny came back to the apartment and we decorated my room. Then we spent a few hours playing board games with Dad and Danny. When Jenny's dad came to pick her up, he and my dad chatted while Jenny and I hung out a little longer in my new space.

Sunday we hiked in the mountains and cooked hot dogs over a fire for lunch. We were in the woods for several hours and ended up behind schedule in the afternoon. Because of the timing, Dad got us some fast food for dinner before he took us home. By that time, I wasn't uncomfortable with him anymore. It was like old times. I was actually a little sad that I had to go back to my mom.

Dad pulled up outside our house, and Danny and I jumped out of the car with a very quick goodbye. We ran inside, and Mom met us as soon as we got in the door. She was extremely happy to see us and hugged us tightly.

"Oh, my babies are home!" she exclaimed. "I missed you both so, so, so much! I was so lonely here all by myself!" She bent down and kissed Danny on the top of his head. And then her face changed.

She frowned and said, "Danny, you're filthy, and you smell like dirt."

"I know," Danny grinned. "We went hiking in the woods, and I was catching toads!"

Mom rolled her eyes and shook her head. "You need to clean up," she told Danny. "Take a bath, and put your clothes in the hamper. We can talk later."

Danny scampered off, still happy. He didn't pick up on Mom's irritation.

"Now," she turned to me and looked concerned. "How was it? You can tell me the truth."

I wondered why she thought I might lie to her. "It was a little weird at first," I said. Mom nodded sympathetically. She reached out and touched my arm before I continued, "But then we went shopping and Jenny came along. We played games, and Dad took us hiking today. I had a good time."

Mom's eyes started to fill with tears.

"What's wrong?" I asked, thinking that maybe something terrible had happened while I was away.

"Oh, nothing," Mom said, sniffling. "I just missed you a lot, that's all."

"I missed you too," I said, giving her another hug. I felt bad about telling her that I had a good time when I knew she had been lonely at home.

Later that night I overheard Mom on the phone with Aunt Tamara. She was filling her in on how our first weekend with Dad went.

"It's completely enraging!" Mom was saying. "Here I am trying to maintain a normal life for them, making sure they brush their teeth and make their beds. Then he swoops in and whisks them away for a weekend of fun. And he took them shopping! Can you believe that? After he didn't have enough money to buy beds for them, and he can't pay for cable. If he can take them shopping to decorate their rooms and buy them new clothes, he should be giving me more money to do the same. It seems I'm the actual parent here."

Aunt Tamara must've had a lot to say because Mom took a long pause.

When she started talking again, she was a little louder. "Well, it doesn't end there," she said angrily. "He hasn't exactly been feeding them well either. He took them out to eat a lot. Today they ate hot dogs and fast food! And you know, he sent me an email tonight and asked to discuss the possibility of him seeing them more often. As if I'd ever allow it! I can't put my kids at risk like that. The supposed nourishment he feeds them will stunt their growth, and his lack of discipline will turn them into criminals. He doesn't even care enough to set boundaries for them!"

I opened my bedroom door and then slammed it shut to let Mom know that I could hear her. I went to bed and put the pillow over my head. I'd had enough. Just when I started to feel better and I had a good weekend, everything was messed up again. I didn't see how this was any better than having my parents fight under the same roof. I also couldn't stop thinking about the things my mom said … about how Dad didn't take care of us, and he didn't care about us. That couldn't be true. *Could it?*

Chapter 3: August

Things around my house started to get busy. Kevin gave us something to think about, other than the divorce, because he was preparing to leave for college. It seemed like every day there was a new thing to add to his list of necessary items for his dorm room. He talked a lot about his schedule, his roommate, his advisor and his student loans. The countdown was on.

One day while Mom wasn't home, he stopped by my room to chat. I was reading a magazine when he poked his head in and asked if he could sit down for a minute. I sat up and made room on the bed.

"So, are you ready to be the oldest kid?" he asked, nudging me with his elbow. "You know, it's a big responsibility. Do you think you can fill my shoes while I'm gone?"

I nodded. "Are you excited?" I asked him.

"Yeah!" he replied. "It's gonna be great to get out of this town and meet people from other places and learn new things ... And meet new girls and go to crazy college parties."

I laughed and looked back toward my magazine.

He was quiet for a second, then said, "So … I heard from your dad."

My head snapped up from the page. I tried not to sound too curious when I asked, "Oh, what did he have to say?"

"It was nice," Kevin began. "He sent me an email and offered to help buy some of my books. He also said that he's really sorry things didn't work out with Mom, that he loves me… and he hopes we can always be friends."

That was nice of Dad. "Did you tell Mom?" I asked him.

He shrugged. "I just got the email this morning. I'm not sure if I'm going to tell her or not. I know for a fact that she thinks he should give her extra money because I'm going to college. But I'm an adult now, so I understand why he chose to deal with me directly."

"She wants Dad to give her money?" I asked. "Why?"

"Because she's going to have to make payments on my school loans," he explained. "She's mad that all this is happening now, and she doesn't think it's fair that she's supporting me by herself."

I didn't know how I should feel about that. "What do you think?" I wanted to know.

"I see her point. Still, I'm not Doug's responsibility. You know? He helped take care of me for a long time, that's true. But I have a father, somewhere, and Mom decided a long time ago that she didn't want him to be in my life. It's not fair for her to put that responsibility on your dad now. Not after the choice she made."

I sighed and looked down. I didn't understand why everything had to be so complicated.

"You know," Kevin said, "I didn't stop in here to talk about this in particular. I came to ask if you wanted anything out of my room while I'm away. Like my TV?"

I laughed. "Sure, I'll take your TV! And your video game system too."

"For real?" Kevin was surprised. "You know, it was made before you were born."

"I know," I responded. "It's different. That's why I like it!"

***

The next time I was supposed to go to my dad's, Mom had other ideas.

"Aunt Tamara and I were scheduled to go to the beauty salon tomorrow, for manicures and pedicures," she told me on Friday afternoon. "But your aunt had to cancel, and now I have two reservations. How about if you come with me?"

"To get my nails done?" I asked.

"Sure," Mom said. "Why not? It'll be nice to get pampered, and we can have some Girl Time."

I loved to paint my own nails but I'd never had a professional manicure before. It sounded like a fun idea. "Well, yeah. OK," I told her. "What time are you going to pick me up from Dad's?"

And then the twist came when she revealed her plan. "I wasn't planning on that, Gina," she explained. "It's a little out of the way for me to go there and pick you up. I thought you'd just stay home tonight, and I can take you there tomorrow afternoon."

I wasn't sure how this kind of thing was supposed to work now that Mom and Dad were split up. I thought maybe I should ask for Dad's permission to spend extra time with Mom, but that seemed silly. She was my mother, after all.

"Oh," I said. I paused slightly before continuing, "Umm, OK. I guess Dad won't mind."

"He better not mind," Mom muttered as she turned to walk out of the room. "I'm the custodial parent."

***

When Dad pulled up, I ran outside and went to his window.

"Hi," he said, smiling. "Where's your bag?"

"I'm not coming tonight," I told him. "I'm going to get manicures with Mom tomorrow, and she said she'll just bring me to your place when we're done."

Dad looked confused and a little hurt. "Well, I guess that's OK. I wish I'd known about this before because I bought tickets to a laser show tonight. I thought we could all go."

I didn't like letting my dad down. Maybe I should have checked with him before I told Mom I'd go with her.

"Can we go tomorrow instead?" I suggested.

Dad thought for a second. "Maybe we can do that," he told me.

"Great!" I kissed his cheek. "Danny will be out soon. He was trying to pick a toy to bring along. I'll see you tomorrow!" I turned and trotted back to the house.

***

Mom and I watched a movie that night. It was the kind that are made to be shown on TV, one that my dad would call a "chick flick."

Mom settled on the couch next to me with a bowl of ice cream. "There are some perks to being separated," she said as she pulled a blanket over her legs. "Your dad used to complain every time I wanted to watch this channel. Now I can watch as often as I want."

I smiled at her. It was nice to be home alone with my mom, knowing that it was just the two of us. Kevin was planning to spend the whole weekend visiting his future roommate, so even he wouldn't be home later.

Mom and I ate lots of ice cream and cookies. We stayed up late. When Aunt Tamara called, Mom told her she couldn't talk because she was "spending quality time with her favorite daughter." I felt special.

The next morning Mom and I set off for the salon, and she let me pick the music in the car. When we got to the spa, we waited in a large room with comfy furniture. There were lots of different kinds of drinks available, and they even had some snack foods. Mom flipped through a magazine, and I sat down with an iced tea. We'd arrived quite early, so I started looking for a magazine as well. And then Mom closed hers and turned to me.

"There's something I need to tell you," she started. "And now probably isn't the best time, but I don't know when the best time is. I didn't want to ruin last night, so …"

I kept quiet, and she took a deep breath before resuming. "I'm going to be putting the house on the market."

I didn't know what she was saying. Luckily I didn't have to ask because she kept talking. "Since your father left us, we all have to make adjustments. Downsizing where we live is one of them. Just like he got a smaller car."

I stared at her. "We're going to move?" I asked.

She nodded.

Although I already knew the answer to my question, I asked it anyway. "Do we have to?"

"Well, it's the best thing," she responded. "Your dad and I are working to untie our assets and pay off our debts, and the house is a big one. If we sell it, we can use the money to pay off my car as well as our credit cards … Oh, but you don't need to worry about that. Let's just say that we're starting a new life, and it's fitting to find a new place to live. Somewhere that doesn't have so many bad memories attached to it. Doesn't that sound like a good idea?"

Bad memories? No! Mine were *good* memories. Our house was where I learned to ride a bike, and it's where Danny learned to walk. It's where we baked cookies and ate them while they were warm. I didn't want to leave! What if I had to change schools? What if we had mean neighbors? What if we couldn't move to a house but had to get an apartment like Dad?

I tried not to cry. I tried not to scream too, but I think my voice came out louder than I'd intended.

"I don't wanna move!"

Mom shushed me. "Unfortunately Gina, this isn't your decision."

I lowered my voice. "What about my friends?" I asked. "And school? You always said we go to an excellent school. Are you going to send us somewhere else?"

"I plan to stay within the same school district," she said. "Maybe we can even move closer to your friends."

"But it's my house! You're taking away my home!" I was so upset that I felt dizzy. Thoughts were whizzing through my head, and I felt like the room was spinning.

"Home is where you make it," Mom said, turning back to her magazine. It was as though she thought she could just turn away from me, and I would stop talking. But I wasn't going to let her ignore me. This was a big deal, and I needed to make her understand.

"How could you take away something that is so important to your children?" I challenged her.

She said nothing. I narrowed my eyes and tried harder.

"How could you let this happen?" I asked. "Don't you care how I feel? Don't you realize how much I've lost? You and your divorce are ruining everything!"

That got a response. Mom straightened up and closed her magazine. She turned to me, and it looked like she might cry, but her voice was even.

"Gina," she began. "The bottom line is that your father doesn't support us as much as he used to. So if you're going to be mad at someone, it should be him. I'd rather not add another layer of paperwork and meetings to this process, but I have no choice right now. I'm sorry this is hard for you. It's hard for all of us." With that, she excused herself and disappeared into the ladies' room.

I sat there, frozen. I wondered if this was the result of Kevin's school loans. It seemed my mom really did need more money.

I didn't have much time to think about it. A long-haired woman dressed in white came to the waiting area and called for us. Mom was just exiting the bathroom and, thankfully, she looked much better than when she'd gone in.

Moving. Money. Lawyers. I needed to get those thoughts out of my head. It was time to relax and try to forget about everything for a while.

***

After our nails had been painted and dried, Mom sent Dad a text message to let him know he could expect me soon. Then she drove me downtown and dropped me off in front of Dad's building. I knew better than to talk about the house or our little fight at the spa. I thanked Mom for the fun I'd had with her and ran through the doors, past the mailboxes, and up the stairs.

When I walked into Dad's apartment, I saw Danny on the couch. He was wearing his new clothes, watching a movie and eating potato chips. Dad walked out of the kitchen to greet me.

"Hey, you finally made it!" he exclaimed. "We've been waiting for you all day."

I suddenly felt my anger about moving return. Danny was wearing new clothes, Dad bought tickets to a laser show, and Mom had to sell her house because Dad wasn't giving her enough money to support us. I didn't plan to be so angry with Dad when I got there. It just happened.

"Mom told me about the house," I blurted out.

"She did? I was hoping we could all sit down and discuss that one together," he offered in response. He looked disappointed.

The more I thought about it, the more upset I became. Everything I'd heard about the divorce was swirling in my brain at once. My anger was growing as I countered with, "You mean you wanted to be there to admit that it's your fault?"

Danny got up off the couch. "What about our house?" he asked. "What's Daddy's fault?"

I turned to Danny. "We have to move out of our house because Daddy decided he'd rather have an apartment and tickets to the laser show," I explained.

"Gina, that's not fair," Dad said. "Do you want to talk about this? Do you want to hear what I have to say?"

"I know enough already," I replied loudly. "I know that Mom has a lot of bills, and she has to pay for everything by herself now. And Kevin is going away to school, and she has to pay for that and you aren't helping her! You always paid for things Kevin needed when you lived with us. You can't do something for years and then just stop all of a sudden. It messes up peoples' lives!" By that time, I was crying, and I ran to my room.

I slammed the door and dove onto my bed. Everything was different. Nothing felt right anymore. My mom was sad or mad most of the time. Dad always seemed to be happy even though the rest of us weren't. Kevin was leaving. In a few weeks I was going to start seventh grade, and I'd always heard that one is the hardest. I was crying so hard that it was difficult to catch my breath. I was sobbing and gasping and screaming and, eventually, I got very tired and fell asleep.

When I woke up a couple hours later, I could smell dinner. I heard Dad in the kitchen. He was telling Danny where the silverware was so he could set the table. Dinner smelled good, which surprised me because my dad wasn't a very good cook. Even though I was curious, I wasn't about to leave my room after what happened earlier. I felt better, but I was still a little mad. And worse than that, I was embarrassed.

I picked up a book and started reading. A few chapters into it, there was a knock on my door. Dad tried to open it, but it was locked.

"Gina, can I come in?" His voice was soft. "I brought you some dinner. You can eat in here, if it will make you feel better. I'd really like for you to eat."

I couldn't deny my growling stomach. I got up and opened the door. "Can we talk?" Dad asked as he handed me a plate of chicken and vegetables.

I nodded and sat down on the floor with my dinner. I was impressed and couldn't wait to dig in. Dad even put cheese on the veggies because he knew that's how I liked them.

"I was hoping things wouldn't happen like this," he said as he sat down next to me on the floor. "I'm sorry that you're going to leave the house. I didn't want that to happen. It's just the way things are. Your mom and I only have so much money between us, and we need to split it between two households now. That means we all have to make some sacrifices. I got a smaller car and an apartment that only has two bedrooms. I sleep on the couch!"

I wasn't sure what Dad wanted me to say about that. "At Mom's house, we don't have potato chips anymore," I mentioned.

Dad sat back and asked, "Yet, your mom paid for a trip to the spa?" A look of shame flashed across his face then and he leaned forward, softening his tone as he continued, "The point is, life is about choices. I chose to spend my money on potato chips and a laser show because I thought it would help you and Danny enjoy yourselves more when you stay here. I want you to be happy when you come to stay with me. Maybe after you move, your mom will buy potato chips again."

He got quiet for a few seconds, and I didn't say anything, so he started talking again. "And about Kevin," he began. "I've talked to your brother about all of this, and he is comfortable with the current arrangements. He's an adult now, and that's why I spoke to him instead of your mom. She doesn't like to talk to me too much these days anyway. We met for pizza after his shift last Wednesday, and everything is fine. I'm still going to help him out a little. However, I'm going to help him directly instead of giving money to your mom. In the end, it will still be less stress on her pocketbook."

Dad took a deep breath and looked at me. "You shouldn't be worried about this," he sighed. "You shouldn't have to know these things. You're twelve years old and you should be having fun with your friends."

I wasn't sure if he wanted me to respond to that. "My friends' lives are so simple compared to mine right now," I told him. "They don't get it."

"And I'm sorry for that. I feel terrible," Dad said. "It shouldn't be that way."

I kept eating and didn't say anything. Dad must've taken a cooking class or something because the food was delicious.

He got up. "I'll give you some privacy. If you feel up to it, please come out and join us. Danny and I would like to take a walk and get some dessert in a little while."

I nodded, and he closed the door.

***

When Dad dropped me and Danny off at home on Sunday night, he came to the door but didn't come in. "Please tell your mother I'd like to speak with her," he told us as we entered the house.

I found my mom dusting in her bedroom and told her Dad was outside. She let out a big sigh and threw her rag on the bed. She quickly walked to meet him on the front porch and immediately asked why he "felt the need to disturb me with your presence instead of calling like a normal person." Sometimes Mom could be really mean.

Dad told her he wanted to talk about me and how much I knew about their situation.

"Well, it's pretty hard to hide the details from her," she started. "Don't you think so, Doug? I mean, really, how am I supposed to sell the house and move without her knowing?"

"You know what I mean." Dad was talking slowly. I could tell he was struggling to stay calm. "You told her it was my fault. She's angry and worried about things that shouldn't concern her. She's only twelve years old."

"It *is* your fault!" she exclaimed, then quickly brought the conversation back to me. "And she is very mature for her age. I personally think that's a good quality. She's wise beyond her years, and she doesn't always need to be treated like a child."

"I don't think she should be stressed out about this," Dad was saying. "I think we should talk to the kids about the positive changes we're making here. We're doing all of this so everything will be better than it was, and they need to understand that."

"Well, that's a pretty hard idea to sell right now," Mom said. "I'm just being honest."

"She's a kid! And you haven't been completely honest with her anyway." Dad's words hit a nerve.

"I am her mother, and I know what is best for my children!" she lashed out at him. "Do not stand on my porch and tell me how to run my life. If you have a problem with the way things are, you can call your lawyer and make an appointment with a judge. Then try to tell him that you and your dirty car, your crappy apartment, and your terrible cooking are what's in the best interest of my kids."

Caught slightly off guard, Dad tried to explain. "I didn't say I wanted them to live with me. I'm only trying to—"

She cut him off in mid-sentence. "Oh no, *of course* you don't want them to *live* with you! That would cramp your style, wouldn't it? Too much responsibility for you, right? You're pathetic."

"Jill, that's not it either. I just … oh, forget about it," I heard a sigh and then Dad's footsteps walking away.

I made a mad dash for the back door so Mom wouldn't discover I'd been listening when she came in the house. I sat down in a chair on the patio. Mom came out a few minutes later with a glass of wine.

"I'm sorry your dad put you in the middle like that," she said.

I looked down at my hands. I was afraid to tell Mom that I was the one who got mad and brought up the situation at Dad's. He didn't put me in the middle. He tried to talk me out of it.

"Next time, you just need to tell him you don't want to talk about those things," Mom was saying. "And if he doesn't listen, call me, and I will come and pick you up so you don't have to deal with it. You can *always* call me to come get you. You know that, don't you?" She moved closer to me and put her hand on my arm.

I nodded again and stood up. "I need to go separate my laundry and clean up my room," I told her. Then I walked back into the house. I needed to escape the tension. Even though Mom was acting nice, I could tell she was still mad, and I didn't want her to get mad at me. Besides, I was already mad at myself. If I hadn't said anything, there wouldn't have been a fight. I remembered when Dad told me he was moving out and he said it wasn't my fault. This time, it was.

***

Later that night I heard my mom on the phone with my aunt. They were discussing the recent events. From my room, I tried not to listen but I couldn't distract myself from Mom's conversation. I tried to think happy thoughts, but I couldn't think of any. In the end, I remembered Mom saying that I was mature and I decided that I should probably take the time to hear how my mom felt about everything. It would help me help be a better daughter for her.

"Well, of course I told her it's because of him. It's the truth!" Mom sounded defensive.

"Yes, and she's very mature. She has a right to know what's going on."

"Well, I told her that she doesn't have to stay there if she's uncomfortable."

"I'm always willing to come and pick her up. I know how he is."

"Yeah, it was nice to get things done around here."

"But she shouldn't have to deal with it. I lived with him long enough to have sympathy for anyone else who lives with him."

As their conversation wore on, I grew more and more confused. I didn't understand as much as I needed to. I wished I could hear what Aunt Tamara was saying, but I knew that if I was caught listening on another line, I'd be in serious trouble. I'd just have to try harder and pay more attention to everything.

***

Dad sent me a few text messages over the next couple weeks. They were short: "thinking about you," "isn't it a great day? I hope you spent it swimming" and "Grandma and Grandpa say 'hi.' They miss you!"

I thought about my grandparents. I missed them too. I missed being carefree at their house and on the cruise ship. Somehow when I was with them, all of my problems disappeared. It was always like that, ever since I was little. I wanted to go to their house and have Grandma make me pancakes and brownies. I wanted to sit at the little table by the big window and watch the birds outside at the feeder. I wanted to sleep in the big soft bed in my dad's old bedroom. If I could just go there, everything would be better. Even if it was only for a little while.

But I couldn't ask for a trip to Grandma and Grandpa's house. There was too much going on. The house was for sale. Kevin was going to leave soon. Danny had been irritable and was acting out a lot. I was helping Mom around the house, and she was teaching me to cook. Besides, I'd heard my mom talking to Aunt Tamara about my grandparents, and she said they were "superficial" and "stuck up." It would hurt my mom's feelings if I told her I wanted to see them. The last thing I wanted to do was hurt my mom on top of everything that she was going through with the divorce.

I thought about my other grandparents, my mom's parents. I'd spent some time with them before, but it was different. Gigi and Poppy worked a lot, and they were always busy. Even when they weren't busy, they were busy. It was hard to relax at their house. They didn't have a bird feeder, and the brownies were never homemade. They always came in a plastic container from the supermarket.

I'd just have to stick it out at home.

***

Two days before Kevin left for school, Mom asked me if I wanted to come along to help him move. Right away, I felt uneasy because it was a weekend I was supposed to be with Dad.

"I think it'll be a good experience for you," Mom told me. "You'll get to see his campus and his dorm. You'll get a taste of college life. It's something you'll need to start thinking about soon."

I thought about how Kevin said he was excited to move and meet people and learn new things. When I thought about myself on a college campus, I felt glamorous, older and mature. I imagined we'd walk and talk about important things and stop in one of those cool coffee shops where everyone has a laptop and a latte. I began to smile.

"It sounds like fun. But what about Dad?" I asked.

Mom scowled. "Don't worry about him. I'm sure he cares about you enough to see that this will be a good experience for you."

I wasn't sure what that meant. I smiled anyway and told Mom that I was up for the trip.

Mom called Dad later that night to talk about Saturday. It didn't take long for her to get angry.

"You?!?!" she yelled. "What about you? This has nothing to do with you! It has to do with your daughter and her education. Her future! I cannot believe how *selfish* you are!"

"No, that's my weekend with them, and we have plans."

"I don't think that's a good idea. We'll be leaving very early on Saturday morning. It's a five hour drive. Don't you remember?"

"I don't know. There's a good chance we'll stop halfway and spend the night."

"Well, that's hardly my problem."

"She wants to go! How could you even think about taking this away from her? It's *important*."

"Too fast? No. It's never too early to start planning for these things."

"Yes, Doug. She should be part of that process."

"Are you forgetting the fact that Kevin is her brother? I know you've abandoned him, but your daughter still cares about him very much."

"Oh, don't make me laugh!"

"Friday?"

"Well, yes, I could use some time alone with him."

"OK. But you'll need to have her home before nine o'clock."

"Early? Oh my ... yeah. OK. Whatever you want."

I heard her sigh and open the refrigerator. I guessed I'd be spending Friday evening with Dad, and he was going to pick me up early. I was right. A few minutes later, Mom called me and Danny to the kitchen to tell us the news.

"Why does Gina get to do all this special stuff?" Danny asked. "It's not fair!"

"Because I'm more mature than you are," I taunted.

Mom shot me a look. "Gina is older, and it's true she has broader interests than you, Pumpkin," she told him. "But that doesn't mean she's any more special than you. How about next weekend you and me leave Gina home, and I'll take you horseback riding?"

Danny nodded excitedly. He'd wanted to ride a horse since he caught a glimpse of an old western movie on TV when he was three years old. Mom always told him it was too dangerous. Now she changed her mind? I didn't get it. I excused myself and went to the computer.

***

Dad picked us up early as planned. As soon as we were settled in the car, Dad asked me what I wanted to do for dinner.

"Since I have to return you so early," he began, "you're the guest of honor."

I thought for a minute and suggested my favorite restaurant, the one with the awesome miniature cheese sticks. Dad and Danny both groaned because they didn't like the food there, and Dad always complained that it was too crowded. But there was no formal objection. After all, I was the guest of honor, and it was my choice.

Being the guest of honor proved to be pretty cool. Dad focused all his attention on me during dinner and then told me I could have whatever I wanted for dessert. I chose a medium-sized sundae with four toppings. I chatted happily about getting Kevin's TV and game system. I told him about my friends and the homeroom teacher I'd been assigned to for the upcoming school year. I didn't think to ask Dad anything about what was going on with him.

Danny kept trying to talk about himself, but Dad told him there would be plenty of time for the two of them to talk tomorrow. For now, they needed to "enjoy the time with Gina while she's here with us."

After dinner, I wanted to walk along the river. We drove back to Dad's apartment and began walking south. There were a lot of wildflowers on the trail. I picked some with the intention of putting them in a vase. Danny looked for turtles, and Dad talked a little bit about some of the upcoming events along the riverfront. The city had planned a street fair and some fireworks displays in the next month. Dad said he hoped he'd be able to take me and Danny. He even said I could bring Jenny and Sarah.

We finished walking around seven o'clock, so we went back to Dad's apartment to relax. While we were there, my grandma called.

"She's here now," Dad said. "I'll put her on the phone."

"Hi, Grandma," I said.

"Hi, Gina! It's so nice to hear your voice," Grandma gushed. "I haven't talked to you in two months."

"I know," I said. "I've been really busy."

Grandma and I had a quick chat. She told me there was a raccoon that had moved onto their property and that Mr. and Mrs. Nelson next door had a pool put in their back yard. She told me that she missed me, and she loved me, and Grandpa did too, and they couldn't wait to see me again. She suggested that we visit for a weekend in the fall. I thought that sounded great, especially if Laurie could be there too. I hadn't talked to Laurie since the day after the cruise. When I was done talking to Grandma, I handed the phone to Dad, and he went into the kitchen. He ducked his head down a little and stood in the corner.

I stayed within earshot and listened to the one-sided conversation. Sometimes, I thought I knew exactly what was being said on the other end of the line. Most of the time, I didn't.

"I know," he said.

"We had a good night. I let her pick what we did."

"What else am I supposed to do?"

"I know that, but I want to make sure she's happy."

"I know you would, but I don't want to make things ugly."

"I know, but they've been through so much. I don't see how additional animosity can make things better for them."

"Hi, Dad."

"Yeah,"

"I know."

"No, I'm not saying that. I just … I don't know. And I shouldn't talk about this now."

"Yes. I have to take her back in about forty-five minutes. How about I call you later? Will you be awake after ten?"

"OK, then."

"I love you too."

"Yes, I will. Goodbye."

Dad came into the living room. "How about a board game before you leave, Gina?" he asked.

Danny suggested dominoes, but I was quick to cut him off.

"Hey," I snapped. "He asked *me* what *I* wanted to do."

Danny looked sad. "I'm going to go play dinosaurs," he mumbled as he shuffled to his room.

"Great!" I smiled and turned toward Dad. "So … how about … chess?"

Dad looked uncertain. "Have you and Danny been getting along OK?"

"Sure," I said, getting up and going into the kitchen. "Except when he acts obnoxious. He can be a real pain sometimes." I grabbed a bag of chips and sat down at the table.

Dad took a deep breath and then seemed to shake off whatever he was thinking about, which was probably his conversation with my grandparents. "OK," he said. "Chess, it is!"

***

The next morning, Mom woke me up while it was still dark outside. I groaned and asked if I could sleep another half hour. She said I couldn't, but I could sleep in the car when we got on the road. I rolled over, then I snuggled down under my blankets again. Mom pulled the covers off me.

"Gina. Now!" she ordered.

I propped myself up and looked out the window. I could tell the sun was going to come up soon. I stood up and stretched. Then I ambled to my dresser and started picking out clothes.

The kitchen smelled like coffee. Aunt Tamara was sitting at the island with a mug when I came into the room. I poured a glass of milk and sat down beside her.

"I didn't know you were coming along," I said.

"Are you kidding?" she asked. "I wouldn't miss my first nephew's trip to college! We are gonna have so much fun, dontcha think?" She nudged me with her elbow.

I smiled, took a sip of milk and then asked where Kevin was. Aunt Tamara told me that he and my mom were still loading the car. A few minutes later, they announced that they were ready and we hit the road.

I napped during most of the drive. I think Kevin did too. I woke up when Mom told us that we were there. I looked out the window and saw lots and lots of green grass. And big trees. And there was a creek. And a pond! And lots of benches and people and really big buildings. I put the window down so I could smell the air. It smelled fresh, definitely different from the air back home. I was impressed already and I hadn't even stepped out of the car.

Kevin's dorm was a madhouse. It didn't match the beautiful scenery I'd seen just a few minutes before. Everywhere, there were people and *stuff*. There were men in orange vests trying to help everyone park and then there were other people wearing blue collared shirts who brought big carts to the parking lot. We got a cart and started loading Kevin's things. When we had one full load, we headed for the building, waited eons for the elevator and then slowly navigated through the hall to Kevin's room, #804. His roommate, JJ, was already there with his parents. The room was tiny and all of us barely fit inside.

"Just dump it all on your bed and go get the rest," JJ said to Kevin. "There's no point in trying to organize anything now." JJ was cute. He had dark wavy hair and bright blue eyes. When he smiled there was a dimple in his right cheek.

We did as JJ suggested and then went back into the hallway to wait again for an elevator. There were too many people there, too many piles of clothes and too many electrical cords trailing behind carts. A bunch of parents had red faces because they'd been crying. I was no longer impressed. I was bored and I was beginning to wish I'd stayed with my dad.

It took a few hours to move all of Kevin's things to his room and then remove the things he decided he didn't want to keep. When Mom and Aunt Tamara took his extra stuff back to the car, I asked if I could stay in the room with Kevin and JJ. Mom said it was OK with her if it was OK with Kevin. And it was OK with him too. I sat down in the wheeled desk chair on Kevin's side of the room. JJ's parents had already left so it was just the three of us. I secretly pretended that I was visiting from another college and that I was JJ's girlfriend and we were going to go to a party later. The guys talked about what was going on around campus that weekend and what they would do the following day. JJ's older brother went to the same college, so he knew a lot about where to go and what to do. I chimed in and talked when I could. Most of the time they talked about things I didn't understand, so I kept quiet and picked at my nail polish.

When Mom and Aunt Tamara came back, they suggested we all go get something to eat— even JJ could come with us. My heart leapt! But Kevin told my mom that they had a lot to do and they thought we should go ahead without them. We all hugged Kevin and wished him luck. He told me to take care of his TV and game system, and I promised I would. Then we left.

I begged Mom to find a coffee shop on campus where we could eat. She said something about those places being too expensive, but Aunt Tamara agreed with my suggestion and said she'd pay for it. She said it would be nice to escape the hustle-bustle and relax somewhere.

We found a coffee shop close to the dorms. I was excited because you could smell it from the street and inside it was dim and there was a corner set up for musical performances. In the back was a big area with lots of seats on the floor— seats from cars! Some were big cushy benches and some were smooth, small, sleek seats from sports cars. I thought they were awesome. Mom and Aunt Tamara complained about having to sit so close to the ground and not having a table to eat over. I was disappointed that the students there weren't studying.

Most of them were there with their parents. I guessed that was because school hadn't started yet.

I ate quickly because I knew Mom and Aunt Tamara wanted to leave. I did too, even though the seats were cool. I was tired and ready to go home. The college scene was nothing like what I thought it would be. There were so many long lines and so many people that it felt like an average tourist attraction.

***

We drove for about three hours that night and then stopped at a hotel. We were all tired and couldn't stand the thought of spending two more hours in the car. When we got up the next morning, we felt refreshed and ready to get on the road.

At home, I felt heavy and sad. The house was quiet and calm. Our dishes from Saturday's breakfast were still in the sink, and Kevin had left one of his hoodies on the couch. I picked it up and took it to his room. Then I went to my room and played an old video game. I wasn't very good at it. I ended up playing for more than an hour before I got hungry and went to the kitchen.

Through the window, I saw Mom sitting on the back patio. She was alone, and she wasn't typing, texting or talking. I decided to join her.

"Hi," she said when I walked outside.

"Hi," I told her.

"How are you doing?" she asked.

"Fine," I said, sitting down.

"I was just sitting here thinking about the time we've spent in this house," Mom said reflectively. She sat back in her chair and sighed. "We have had a lot of good times here. You and me and Danny and Kevin..." Her voice faded, and she started to cry.

I didn't know what to do. It was scary to see my mom start crying like that because she wasn't mad. She was *sad*. And that was a different kind of crying altogether. When she was mad, I could leave her alone. But I couldn't do that now.

"Mom? Are you OK?" I asked softly as I reached out to her.

She nodded and didn't say anything. Then she took a deep breath and tried to talk, but she was still crying.

"I,"

"I'm"

"I'm so g—"

"I'm so glad you're here, Gina." She looked at me, and her eyes were wet and red. "I don't know what I'd do without you right now. Your dad is gone, Kevin is gone, the house is—"

She broke into sobs again. I wanted to cry too, but I wouldn't let myself. She needed me too much. She'd just said so.

"Mom, it's gonna be OK," I told her. "Kevin isn't gone. He's just at school. You can call him right now if you want. And I'm here. And Danny will be back in a few hours. And it's just like you said before about the house. It will be nice to move somewhere that doesn't have so many bad memories attached to it."

Mom kept sniffling, but I could tell she was calming down.

"Thanks," she said, forcing a smile. "Thanks for being here for me when I needed you."

"Uh … no problem," I said, sitting back in the chair.

That night I hugged Henry-The-Stuffed-Bunny while I lay in my bed and thought about everything that was happening. I thought about how far we'd come in the two months since my parents decided to divorce. I thought about the fact that I had two bedrooms. I thought about my grandparents. I wondered where I'd spend the holidays now that Mom and Dad weren't together. It seemed like Danny and I had two different families now: one with my mom and one with my dad.

I thought about Danny and how he was too young to understand things the way I did. He was needy and couldn't take care of himself. He was just another thing to stress my mom out. Every time he asked for help opening a new bottle of juice, I could feel her bristle because he was interrupting her.

Mom needed all the help she could get. I knew she was struggling. She'd started referring to herself as a "single parent" and talking about how she had to be two people at the same time. She had a hard time keeping the house as clean as she used to, and I knew that bothered her a lot. I was worried about her, especially after her breakdown earlier in the day. I didn't want her to be alone or to feel like it was too much for her. We needed her more than ever.

I thought about my dad and how easy everything was for him. He wasn't around to fight with Mom. He also wasn't around to help her. He only had to worry about me and Danny every other weekend—only four days each month! He was probably saving a lot of money on food. All he had to do was go to work and come home. He didn't have to deal with cleaning the house so the realtor could give tours. He didn't have to schedule those visits with the real estate office. He didn't even have a lawn and flower beds to take care of.

I also tried to decide how I felt about my dad. He wasn't around, so we weren't as close as we had been before he moved out. We used to go for hikes and shoot hoops outside and lately there'd been no time for that. He didn't even know for sure that I was in my bed at that moment. And he kept fighting with Mom. I was mad at him for making her angry. I was upset that he didn't want me to go to Kevin's school, even if it did turn out to be a waste of my time. Mom had said he'd let me go if he cared about me … and then he didn't want me to go. I guessed all of our time apart had an effect on him too. Maybe he didn't love me as much as he did when he lived at home. Maybe we were just "growing apart." That was what my mom told the neighbors about her and my dad. I guessed that could happen with me too.

Chapter 4: September

The evening after the first day of school, Dad called the house. Danny answered the phone and talked first. He happily babbled about his teacher, Mrs. Lewis, who used to be a dolphin trainer. He talked about how much longer school takes in first grade versus kindergarten. He even told Dad what they were serving in the cafeteria and what color shoes he wore.

When it was my turn, I kept it short. I made sure I didn't tell Dad anything that I hadn't told Mom. I knew she was listening, although she was pretending to read the paper. Dad said he wanted to know all about my day. He said that he always heard seventh grade was the hardest and asked if I thought it was going to be difficult. I told him that everything was fine. My locker worked, and I had two classes with Sarah, study hall with Jenny, and lunch with both of them. I also told him that the bus ride was shorter, and the bus driver was nicer than the one I had in sixth grade.

Dad told me a little bit about what he'd been doing lately. He said he was busy at work and that he bought some artwork for the walls in the apartment. He also told me that he found some bikes for me and Danny at a flea market, so we could take rides along the river. And he said that my Uncle Skip and his girlfriend, Ginger, were going to have a baby. In the spring, I was going to have a new cousin!

I felt good when I got off the phone, but I tried not to act too happy because Mom was in a bad mood. I told her the news and was careful not to sound excited. She listened patiently and then nodded. She asked me if Skip and Ginger were going to get married. I told her I didn't know. She shook her head and moved her eyes back to the paper. I took that as my cue to stop talking about Dad's family.

***

A few days later, I heard Mom on the phone. I didn't know who she was talking to. She suddenly sounded very curious about something.

"Oh, really?"

"Was she young?"

"Well, that's typical."

"I wonder what he thinks he's doing. Legally, he's still married."

She was talking about my dad, I was sure of it. My dad and … someone else. I walked to the door of my room so I could hear a little better.

"Yes, it just makes him look desperate. That's all."

"And you don't know who she is?"

"This is going to be hard for the kids. He's obviously not thinking about them."

"No, it's good that you called. I'd rather know than be made a fool of all over town."

"Yes, I will. You too."

"Thanks. Buh-bye."

After that, Mom's actions got louder. Her footsteps became heavier, and I could hear her moving things around in the kitchen. I heard her pull out a chair and sit down. Then I heard her on the phone again.

"So. I hear you're dating."

"I have my sources, Doug. That's really none of your business. When were you planning to tell me?"

"It *absolutely* has something to do with me. I am the mother of your children!"

"And thank God for that! Of course, I'm certain I would have done a better job. I would have raised you to be more considerate of others."

"How do you figure?"

"You were parading around town in a convertible! Did you think people wouldn't notice? Did you think nobody would tell the kids?"

"Don't lie to me. I think they have a right to know what's going on in your life."

"This isn't about me and you. You really need to think about other people from time to time. Why are you so selfish?"

"Why not? Is she there with you right now?"

"How old is she anyway? And does she realize that you have a wife and kids?"

"Yes, it *is*. Your children are going to be positively distraught over this, and they're going to want answers."

"Oh, what, because you're not a father when they're not with you? You should be thinking about them with every action you take!"

"Yes, it is. That's why I called to discuss it with you."

"NO! I am talking about our kids!"

"Is this why you left, Doug? Is she the reason, huh? Did you have her waiting in the wings for you to finally be free of your ball and chain?"

"Because you want someone to make you feel young and attractive. I understand. That doesn't mean you don't have responsibilities to other people."

"What is she, like twenty-five?"

"Just tell me the truth. I deserve to know these things because we have *children*! Does she have children? How much does she even know about kids?"

"I don't think so."

"Well, I'm not the one playing the field right now, am I? I'm the one staying home to raise Gina and Danny."

"It's about being responsible."

"Your daughter is more responsible than you are."

"I told you. I called to discuss this with you because our children are going to want to know details. I don't know why you aren't cooperating."

"Yes, it is!"

"What? When they meet her? No!"

"How long before? And what about me? I'd like to know what kind of person you're exposing my kids to."

"You haven't thought this out at all, have you?"

"Well, I hope she's pleased with her decision. You're a horrible man, Doug. I don't know why I ever married you. You don't care about anyone but yourself, and if we didn't have— Hello? HELLO?"

Mom had been pacing around the kitchen, but she stopped. She was quiet for a minute, and then I heard her footsteps getting closer. I dove for my bed and opened up a book. She knocked on the door.

"Yeah?" I called from the bed.

"Gina, we need to talk," she told me. I was always amazed at how Mom seemed to think I couldn't hear her when she was on the phone. Especially since there were times when it sounded like she was being extra loud because she wanted me to know what was going on.

"OK." I figured it was better to play dumb and let Mom lead.

She came in and sat down on the side of the bed. "Your father is seeing someone," she said gently, looking into my eyes.

I looked away. I didn't have to pretend to be surprised. When she said the words, it all came together, and it was as if I was realizing it for the first time. I didn't know what to say, or do, or feel.

"Who?" I asked.

Mom took a deep breath. "I don't know. I tried to get some answers for you, Sweetie, but your dad refused to discuss it. He wouldn't even admit it to me. All I know is that she has red hair and drives a convertible. I think she's probably a great deal younger than he is, and I don't think she has any children of her own."

I sat there, frozen. There was nothing I could say. It seemed like Mom was expecting me to scream or cry, but I just sat there.

"OK," I finally said. There wasn't anything else I could say. Mom didn't have any information. She couldn't answer my questions, even if I knew what to ask.

Then I wondered how my mom felt. She'd expected a serious talk with me, and it wasn't happening.

"Has he been seeing her a long time?" I asked.

Mom shook her head and sniffed. "I'm not sure."

I thought she might cry again, like she did after Kevin went to college. I braced myself and tried to think about what I would do if that happened. But she didn't cry. Instead, she seemed to pull herself together.

"Are you OK?" she asked me.

"Yeah, I guess," I replied. "I mean ... I think it's kinda soon. But ... I don't know."

"I'm so sorry he's doing this to you," she told me. "And he wouldn't tell me anything. He doesn't understand how much he's hurting you."

I didn't say anything. Mom took a deep breath and shook her head, "Maybe he was waiting to see you this weekend," she thought out loud. "Maybe you'll meet her then."

I still didn't say anything.

"Are you OK?" she asked again.

I nodded. Mom patted me on the shoulder and reminded me that I could talk to her if I wanted to talk and that she would always pick me up if I didn't want to stay with Dad.

After she left, I called Jenny.

"My dad has a girlfriend," I told her.

"So?" she asked.

"So? Like ... why does he have a girlfriend? My mom isn't seeing anyone."

Jenny sighed. "Look," she said. "My dad goes on dates all the time."

"He does?"

"Yeah. Duh. He's a single guy! Sometimes I meet them. Most of the time, I don't. My dad is really cool about it. So far, he hasn't met anyone he wants to live with or marry or anything."

"I feel bad for my mom," I told her.

"Why?" she asked. "Your mom is a big girl. She can take care of herself."

"I don't know. She seems upset. She called my dad and wanted to know all about this woman, but my dad wouldn't tell her anything."

Jenny laughed. "She did *what*? I can't imagine my parents calling each other to ask who they're dating! My mom doesn't care what my dad does."

"She wanted to find out for me," I told her.

"Why do you need to know? And *what* do you need to know? How did you find out about this anyway?"

"Someone called and told my mom." This conversation wasn't going quite the way I expected. "I guess whoever it was saw him with someone. My mom said she has red hair and drives a convertible."

"She sounds like fun!" I could tell Jenny was still smiling.

"I think my mom thinks she's immature."

"I don't know why your mom cares," Jenny went on. "Your parents are getting divorced. That means they are going to see other people and maybe even marry someone else someday."

"I guess," I said. "It just seems so soon."

"This is not a big deal," Jenny assured me. "It just sounds like gossip. Your dad's a cool guy. I'm sure he'd tell you if he thought it was important."

Jenny was right. I didn't have any facts and since my dad didn't tell my mom anything, maybe there was nothing to tell. Maybe my mom was overreacting to the whole thing.

Jenny and I talked a little longer before we hung up. I was glad to have a friend who knew all about divorce. I felt better knowing that she didn't think this was anything to get upset about. But at the same time, it was a big deal to me because I'd never been through it before. And still, if it was all just gossip … I didn't know what to think. My mom was always telling me not to spread gossip and not to believe it. And that's what she was doing! She even called my dad and yelled at him about it. Even though she said she was doing it for me ... I wished I didn't know any of it. It was going to be three more days before I saw my dad, and it would bother me until then.

Later that night, Mom called Aunt Tamara and told her about The Girlfriend. At first Mom sounded angry.

She said it was Deanna, an old friend from the gym, who called and told her the news. She talked about the red hair and the convertible and how The Girlfriend sounded "hopelessly immature" and that Dad was "hugely inconsiderate." I don't know what Aunt Tamara was saying at the time, but whatever it was, it made Mom get really quiet. Then she started to cry.

"I don't know. I just … I don't know."

"Well, no. I don't think so. I'm getting used to it."

"I don't know how he can do that. I can't even think about those things right now!"

"Yes, I know they are."

"Yes, I'm glad he's gone."

"I feel sick."

"Yes."

"I could if I wanted to."

"I don't know! I don't want to eat anything. I don't even want to try to sleep."

"But how could he do this to us?" Mom started sobbing harder.

"How could he leave us like this? It's so much of a struggle just to get out of bed in the morning, and now he has to throw *her* in my face too?" She took a minute to breathe and cry some more.

"I feel bad for the kids."

"He's supposed to be their father, not the boyfriend of some young tramp!"

"I don't get his priorities. It destroys me to know what he's doing to them."

"Oh, no. She better not!"

"If she thinks she can walk right into my family and befriend my children, she's got another thing coming."

"I am their mother! She is nothing. NOTHING! I gave birth to them. I raised them. They are *my* kids!"

"Oh, yeah? Then where is he now, huh? Shacking up with her, right? He doesn't qualify to be a dad! Dads are … there, with their children."

After hearing all that, I no longer thought she was overreacting to The Girlfriend. I could tell that it was a big deal. Mom couldn't eat or sleep while Dad was out showing off!

How could he do this to us? I wondered. *Doesn't he realize how difficult things are?*

I guessed he didn't because he wasn't there to see it. Mom said real dads are there for their kids. What did that say about my dad? I started to feel sick, and then I started to cry. I kept it quiet because I didn't want Mom to hear me. I felt alone. My parents had their own issues, Danny was oblivious and my friends didn't get it. I cried until my pillow was wet and my muscles were sore. Then, sometime after midnight, I fell asleep.

***

On Friday, when it was time for me to go with my dad, I didn't want to. I was nervous about The Girlfriend. I was angry at him for upsetting Mom. I was sad that he didn't want to be my full-time dad anymore. Even though Mom had pulled herself together since her conversation with Aunt Tamara, I was worried about her and didn't want her to be alone. I also didn't want to start any more problems between my parents.

"Can I stay home?" I asked Mom. "I don't feel good."

"You don't?" she asked, putting her hand on my forehead. "You don't feel warm."

"My stomach feels funny," I told her. "I just don't want to see him."

"Oh." I could tell by Mom's face that she understood. "Isn't this your chance to get some answers to your questions? You can tell him how you feel."

I shook my head and looked down. "I don't want to. I don't feel good, and I don't want to think about it."

"Gina, this is your weekend to see him."

"But Mom, you said I didn't have to stay and I could always call you if I wanted to come home. Can't I just stay here with you? Please?"

Mom was quiet for a moment, and I could tell she was thinking. She shook her head. "I don't have a good feeling about this."

"Please?" I asked again. "I also have a lot of homework to do. I won't get in your way. I just don't want to see him. Not now. Not after what he did. Please, Mom?" Tears came to my eyes.

Her shoulders slumped. She looked down and shook her head again. "Oh … OK. I guess it's alright. I'll speak to your father when he gets here."

When Dad pulled up, I hid in my room. I did sneak a peek out the window to see if he was in his own car and if anyone else was with him. He was alone in his car. Everything seemed normal. Danny ran outside and dove into the back seat as fast as he could. He didn't understand anything that was going on.

Mom followed Danny. She stood very tall and walked with a lot of confidence. Dad got out of the car and met her at the end of the walkway. I moved away from the window so he wouldn't see me. At first I couldn't tell what they were saying, but it didn't take long before Mom raised her voice enough for me to hear her. Dad responded so quietly, I couldn't hear him.

"She's angry at you, Doug. You let her down."

"Well, excuse me for thinking your children have a right to know what their father is up to."

"No. I told you, she is very upset, and she doesn't want to see you. She's absolutely sick about this, and you should be too after everything you've done to her."

"Me? Oh, that's real mature. If it's my fault, then why is she mad at you?"

"Oh, you have that much money to spend in court? Then how about you pay my lawyer fees as well? It's only fair after the pain you've caused my family!"

"Well, you don't act like it."

Dad raised his voice a little bit, but I still couldn't make out the words. Then he shouted, "Gina, I love you! I'll call you later, Honey!"

After that, I heard the car door slam shut, and he drove away.

Mom came to my room a few minutes later. "OK, you win," she told me.

I got up and gave her a hug. "Thanks, Mom," I said.

"You better thank me. You know your dad thinks this is all *my* fault? He's trying to blame me for how you feel. Isn't that ridiculous?"

I nodded. It wasn't fair for my dad to put my mom in the middle and blame her. She was only trying to help me. He really was selfish, and I was glad I didn't have to see him.

***

Later that night, Aunt Tamara and a bunch of friends arrived at our house. They brought a few bottles of wine and a bunch of food with them.

Mom was surprised and happy to have company. There was a lot of squealing and hugging because she hadn't seen some of her old friends in a long time. Aunt Tamara got some wine glasses out of our cupboard and gave one to each woman. Then she pulled the cork on the first bottle and made sure all the glasses were full.

"To freedom and friendship!" My mom and her friends giggled as they clinked their glasses. I thought they were acting awfully goofy for grown women. They looked like me and my friends, except they were allowed to drink alcohol.

It was obvious that Mom and I were not going to be enjoying a quiet evening followed by a movie on the couch. That was disappointing. I left the commotion and went to my room to play video games.

About an hour later, I came to the kitchen for a snack. Mom and her gaggle of girlfriends were seated around the table. I walked past them to the fridge.

"So, Gina, you're taking a night off from your dad's?" asked Deanna, the woman who told my mom about The Girlfriend.

"He's a jerk," I said, pouring a glass of grape juice. Immediately, I felt my face get hot. I was worried that Mom would yell at me because I wasn't supposed to say mean things about anyone, let alone my father.

There was a brief moment of silence and then Julie, another friend from the gym, began to cackle. "Well, her mama didn't raise no fool," she laughed.

I looked up and was surprised to see the women at the table laughing. Even my mom was smiling. It was the happiest I'd seen her in a long time.

"That's right," Mom said, gesturing for me to come over to her. I did, and she wrapped her arms around me and pulled me into her lap. "That's my girl!"

She looked at me and stroked my hair as she continued her praise. "And I don't know what I'd do without her. She has been a big help to me these last few months." Mom smiled at her friends who grinned back at her.

Maggie chimed in with her southern accent, "Y'all look so much alike." She turned to my mom. "She's beautiful just like you. Thank goodness she didn't get the ugly genes from Doug's side of the family."

That stung a little bit. It was true that I looked a lot like my mom, but when I was little, I looked like my dad. As a matter of fact, our baby pictures were nearly identical. And I didn't think anyone in my dad's family was ugly. I wanted to tell Maggie that *she* was ugly, but I kept my mouth shut.

Mom gave me another squeeze, and I hugged her back. She looked proud and that made me happy.

Now the conversation turned to how much better off my mom was since she and my dad separated. Rachel, another guest, told my mom she even looked younger since she "took out the trash."

I began to feel a little out of place and uncomfortable. I excused myself and went back to my room.

"She's matured a lot since we separated," I could hear Mom saying. "She understands it all, and she's handled everything like a champ. I am so proud of her!"

Part of me wanted to stay in the kitchen. They were having a good time and said such nice things about me, even if they were saying nasty things about Dad. But I knew it was Mom's time with her friends. I wasn't even supposed to be home. I was supposed to be with "the trash."

***

A couple hours later, Mom came to my door and asked if I wanted to come downstairs and watch a movie. Her eyes looked funny, and she was extra giggly.

"Did you finish the wine?" I asked.

"Just about!" she laughed, then hiccupped. "I think Julie is downing the last of it now."

"Are they going to drive home?" I wanted to know. I was thinking about all the ads I'd seen on TV about the dangers of drunk driving.

Mom looked serious. "No, Gina. We're going to have a little slumber party here tonight. And you don't need to worry about that. My friends and I are adults, OK? We know how to drink like adults."

I nodded and told her I'd join them in a few minutes.

When I emerged from my room, I caught a whiff of freshly popped popcorn. I could hear everyone in the living room talking about movies and celebrities. I walked into the room and sat down on the couch next to my mom. She put her arm around me and wrapped a blanket around us. I felt safe and comfortable.

The movie lasted almost two hours, and it was so good that we couldn't stop talking about it when it was over. We sat up and talked and ate and drank coffee (the kind without caffeine) until almost three o'clock in the morning. My mom's friends told me lots of beauty secrets about conditioning my hair with mayonnaise and putting cucumber slices over my eyes. Mom and I talked about having a spa night at home the next evening. I was having a great time and I couldn't wait to tell my friends about my night.

***

The next day everyone slept late and then we made breakfast together. My job was to dip slices of bread in a bowl of whisked eggs to make French toast. Mom put on some music while we were cooking, and we sang and danced.

When breakfast was over, we cleaned up our mess and that's when our guests started packing their stuff to leave. I'd had a lot of fun the night before and was disappointed to say goodbye. I wondered if that was what all divorced women did while their kids were away.

Just as Aunt Tamara was pulling out of the driveway, the phone rang. Mom checked the caller ID and then frowned as she answered, "Hello?" She paused for a second and then said, "No, you must have the wrong number." She didn't wait for the person on the other end of the line to respond. She just hung up, and then I saw her switch the ringer setting to silent.

"Wrong number," she said, turning to me. "The guy didn't even speak English. I'm sure he didn't understand me, and he might call back."

I just shrugged.

"Hey, let's go do something," Mom suggested. "Do you want to take a walk in the park?"

Mom didn't have to ask me twice. I thought it was a terrific idea.

It was a beautiful fall afternoon. The sun was shining, the birds were singing, and there were many squirrels out and about in the park. While we walked, Mom filled me in on how things were going. She told me that there was an offer submitted on the house, and they were currently in "negotiations." She also said that there was a house she was interested in. She promised to drive past it on our way home so I could see what it looked like.

We talked about the divorce too. Mom said that she had a good lawyer who was fighting hard for us. I wasn't sure what that meant, but I nodded my head and told her I was glad to hear it. She said my dad's lawyer was not as passionate about the case and that made it hard to get anything accomplished. I didn't know what that meant either. Mom was hoping to have everything done by the end of the year, but since my dad and his lawyer weren't cooperating, it would probably take longer. She sounded disappointed about that, which confused me. I thought she was upset that my dad left. I didn't know why she wanted the divorce to happen faster than it was.

I needed her help to understand. "Are you happy about the divorce?"

Mom thought for a minute. "Well, yes," she said, finally. "I *am* happy about the divorce. Especially after the good time we had last night. I'm ready to get on with my life and start having fun again."

"That's good," I told her.

"I was unhappy with your dad for a long time," she went on. "And now I don't have to be miserable anymore."

Again, I thought about our life before my parents separated, and I remembered a lot of good times. I thought about holidays and birthdays and remembered Mom and Dad laughing at the funny things Danny used to say when he was younger. I wondered if all those smiles had been fake. Were my parents just pretending all those years?

"Dad told me he wanted to make things better," I said.

"Well, he certainly seems better. Doesn't he?" She looked uncomfortable. "And I deserve at least as much happiness as he does. After all, I'm working harder than he is."

I was pretty sure Mom wasn't talking about her job. She meant that she had more responsibilities. I'd heard her talking to Aunt Tamara about that. She thought my dad was on vacation from being an adult.

Mom talked more about the things she was dealing with. She told me about her lawyer bills and how she planned to use money from selling the house to pay them. She said that Danny and I were her number one priority and that she was doing everything she could to keep us safe and secure. She apologized about not getting me more new clothes for school. She said the child support from my dad wasn't enough to cover everything I needed.

I felt like an adult walking along the trail with my mom and listening to her tell me about grown-up issues. I was learning a lot, and it helped me put some of the pieces together so I could understand things I'd heard people talk about. I felt like my mom wasn't just my mom. She was a friend. She wasn't someone who was going to yell at me and tell me to clean my room. She was someone who could confide in me. She trusted me to listen to her problems, and that made me more than just her daughter.

"I'm so proud of you," she told me. "When all of this started to happen, I was concerned about you. I was afraid you'd fall apart and you wouldn't understand. But I should've known better. You're a brilliant young woman and I had nothing to worry about. I can really count on you."

I was beaming. I was so glad I stayed home and didn't go to my dad's that weekend. I would have missed out on so much!

***

The following Wednesday, Mom was in an awful mood. She complained that the dishes weren't clean enough and that Danny hadn't picked up his toys from the night before. She muttered to herself as she stomped from room to room. Danny and I knew it was best to stay out of her way.

I decided to cook dinner to give Mom some time to relax. After we finished eating, she went to talk on the phone in her bedroom. I was worried about her, but I wanted to make sure the kitchen and dining room were clean before I tried to find out what the problem was.

"Help me clear the table," I told Danny.

As we moved dishes from the table to the sink, I asked why it seemed like he didn't care what was going on with our parents.

"What do you mean?" he responded.

"Well, you don't seem to care. Like now, Mom might be crying in her room and all you care about is getting your chores done so you can go play. You're not worried about Mom. You never even ask what's going on with the divorce."

Danny shrugged. "Daddy told me not to worry," he said. "He told me that him and Mommy are dealing with a lot of grown-up things and sometimes they have bad days, and I shouldn't worry because they still love me."

Geez, Dad sure had a way of turning a mountain into a molehill. I couldn't believe he made it all sound so simple! Danny didn't understand everything that was going on, and he didn't know anything about Dad's girlfriend. He was having the easiest time out of all of us. And I thought divorce was supposed to be hardest for the little kids.

"So you don't care why Mom is upset?" I asked him.

Danny shrugged again. "Mommy will feel better soon. She always does."

"And you're just going to ignore her? You're gonna go play like nothing is wrong?" I was beginning to feel irritated.

"Daddy says everything will be OK. He told me that Mommy might be upset sometimes, but I shouldn't be upset about it. He said sometimes she needs to be alone."

I sighed. Of course Dad would say that! He wasn't worried about anything either. He didn't care that we were selling our home. He didn't care that Mom was probably crying at that moment. He didn't care about the money we didn't have. All he cared about was having fun with his new girlfriend. And spoiling Danny ... he must've cared about that too because Danny always had a good time when he went to Dad's. But Dad didn't care about me. He didn't care about me because I was at home caring about Mom. Apparently Dad didn't think anyone should care about her. That was obvious from what Danny said.

The more I thought about it, the angrier I got. I was so mad, I wanted to scream and throw the dishes, but of course I didn't do that. I told Danny to go ahead and play, since that was his priority. I would finish cleaning the kitchen because I was the one who was mature and responsible and willing to help. I didn't need Danny. Danny didn't care about anyone else. He was just like Dad— selfish.

A little later, Mom got off the phone and called me and Danny to the living room. She told us that our house was officially under contract, that new people were going to move in the following month, and we needed to start packing.

I felt tears come to my eyes, and I held them back because I knew this was the reason for Mom's bad mood. I didn't want to cause any more stress.

Danny started to cry immediately. "Where are we going to go?" he wailed. "Will we have to live on the streets or in the car like the Russel Family?" The Russels were some people Danny saw in a movie. The father had lost his job, and they were kicked out of their house. They had to sleep in their car.

Mom shook her head and sat next to Danny so she could put her arms around him. "No," she told him as she rocked him back and forth. "No, we won't have to live on the street. As a matter of fact, I found a new house for us to live in, and it's very close to your school."

Danny sniffed and wiped his eyes. "Why didn't you tell me that first?" he wanted to know.

My little brother was right, Mom probably should have told us the good news first. It would've made the bad news easier to handle.

"Is it the one you showed me last weekend?" I asked her.

She nodded. "It is. Danny, would you like to see the house I picked out for us? We could drive over there now. If you'd like, we can stop and get ice cream to celebrate."

I didn't feel much like celebrating, but I went along with it anyway. The new house was smaller, and it was attached to another house on one side. There was no front yard, and the parking area was in the back. There was no garage, so we'd get rained or snowed on when the weather was bad. The only good thing about it was that it was closer to Sarah's house, and I could ride my bike to visit her.

Mom called Diane, the real estate lady, and made arrangements for us to see the inside of the new house that night. We parked in the back and entered the back door into the kitchen. It smelled funny. It wasn't like our kitchen at home, which always smelled like apple pie because of the air fresheners that Mom used. The new kitchen was smaller than ours, and the counter tops were a different material.

The kitchen had a doorway that led to a living room that was very dark. The walls were painted deep red, and the carpet was brown. I felt like I was in a cave, even though there was a big window on one side. I took in the rest of the view and saw that the living room stretched all the way to the front door. That's when I realized that there wasn't a dining room. I wondered where Mom was going to put our big table and the china cabinet, but I knew better than to ask too many questions in front of Diane. That would embarrass Mom.

We went upstairs to see the bedrooms. Mine was the first one, right at the top of the steps. We filed in. The two big windows reminded me of Dad's apartment. The walls were beige, and the carpet was pink. There was a ceiling fan in the middle of the room and a closet that wasn't as big as the one at home.

I imagined having my friends over and all of us staying up late and sleeping in that room. I imagined my bed in the middle with the headboard between the windows and my dresser to the right of the doorway. I thought about putting the TV in the corner near the closet, and my bookshelves on the opposite wall. While I was at it, I imagined other things too. I imagined things I didn't have, like bean bag chairs, a fuzzy yellow rug, a new nightstand, and a bedside lamp. I decided the room had a lot of potential.

"Go take a closer look in the closet," Mom suggested.

I stuck my head in the door and looked to the left and then to the right. There was a hole in the wall, down in the corner. It was big enough to crawl through, so I did. It led me to the next room!

"Where am I now?" I shouted to everyone who was still in my bedroom.

They joined me a few seconds later. Danny crawled through the hole, and Mom and Diane came in the regular door.

"This room is going to be our family room," Mom said. "We'll probably store a lot of stuff in here, including a lot of toys. And when Kevin is home, this is where he will sleep.

It was a small room with no closet and only one window. I thought it was cool that there was a secret passage that led there from my room, and I was glad that it wasn't going to be Danny's room.

We went to Danny's room next. His bedroom had a hardwood floor and light blue walls. He was excited about the floor because it would be easier to operate his remote-control cars on it. The size of the small closet didn't bother him at all. Mom asked if he thought he'd be happy there. He responded by doing a little dance in the center of the room.

Mom's room was the biggest, and it even had a little balcony that looked out over the back yard. I imagined being with Mom in that room, sitting on her bed, and letting her braid my hair while Danny was away at Dad's.

The bathroom was at the other end of the hallway, and it was our last stop. It was small. There was no linen closet. The walls were covered with mint-green tile. There was only one sink. The mirror was tiny and so high on the wall, I could barely see my face in it.

That was when I started to cry. The newness had worn off, and I realized that we were taking a huge step down from the house we had. I let my head droop, walked out of the room, and went down the steps. I found the door to the basement and went down those stairs, hoping to find something better. The basement smelled damp and was full of cobwebs. The light was dim, but I could see the electrical box and the hot water heater in a corner to my left. The washer and dryer were on my right. I wondered if I would come to the basement in the future when I was upset. I tried to imagine actually living in that house. I imagined getting ready for school in that tiny bathroom and eating breakfast in that smelly kitchen. I thought about Kevin coming home and sleeping in the little room. I thought about Danny playing in that room and remembered that he would have a secret passage into my closet. I'd have to keep my closet door locked.

I heard footsteps above my head, so I called out to let Mom know where I was. The crew joined me in the basement a few minutes later. Again, Danny was excited to see a big cement floor so he could play with his cars. He wanted to set up a racetrack down there— in that filth, with the cobwebs! I couldn't believe him. Once again, he had no clue what was going on. He didn't understand that there was another family on the other side of the wall, and we'd have to be quiet so we wouldn't disturb them. He didn't care that there was no garage. All he cared about was himself and his toys.

On the way home, Mom noticed how quiet I was. When she asked why, I told her that I was upset about having to move, but that I understood we didn't have a choice.

"Gina, the truth is we could stay in our house," she told me. "But I don't think you would be very happy under the new circumstances. I wouldn't be able to afford a lot of the things you're used to. There would be no money for Christmas or birthday presents and no vacations." She laughed, "I think I'd have to shop in the thrift stores."

I nodded. I knew Mom was doing the best she could with what she had. I knew that Dad wasn't giving her enough money and she had to make sacrifices. Big sacrifices, like our house.

"I like the new house!" Danny exclaimed from the back seat.

"Well, I'm glad to hear that," Mom said, looking relieved. "I think this is a happy new beginning for all of us."

I bit my tongue. Perhaps some of us were happier than others.

***

When it was time to go to my dad's again, I refused. I was still upset about his girlfriend and the house. Besides, I'd had so much fun at home with Mom last time, I was secretly hoping for another slumber party. This time I would join the party instead of hiding in my room.

I couldn't tell how Mom felt when I told her I wasn't going with my dad. She didn't smile or scowl at me. Her face was sort of blank, and she didn't say anything at first.

I didn't beg like a little girl this time. I was adamant, like an adult would be. "I'm not going," I said again. I even listed my reasons: He hurt my family. He's sneaking around with some other woman … and I haven't even seen him in a month! I concluded my justification with, "I feel creepy when I think about going to his apartment. That's not my *home*."

Mom let out a sigh. "You'll have to tell him yourself," she told me. "Your dad thinks I'm keeping you here on purpose. I'll support you, but you need to be honest with him about the choice you're making."

"Fine. I'll call him right now." I reached for the phone. I dialed Dad's number and he picked up on the second ring.

"Hi, it's Gina," I said.

"Hey there!" I could tell Dad was smiling. He sounded happy to hear from me, and I felt a little guilty about why I was calling.

"Umm, I'm not going to see you this weekend either," I said quickly.

"Again?" he asked. "Why not?"

"Because," I began, suddenly feeling sick in my stomach. "I don't want to. I'm mad at you for messing up my life and fighting with Mom." I hated disappointing him. I started to cry, but I pressed on. I thought about what I was saying and immediately I felt angry. "You're selfish and irresponsible. You abandoned us, and I don't want to see you!"

Dad didn't say anything for a long time. I sat there and held my breath, waiting. When he did speak, I could tell that he was trying not to cry.

"Can we talk?" he asked. "Maybe I can work it out with your mom, and you and I can have dinner alone tonight. I didn't abandon you, Gina. I miss you and think we need to spend some time together."

"No, I don't want to."

"Please?" Dad's voice sounded fragile. He was begging me like I had begged Mom two weeks earlier. He sounded like a little kid. "Please, talk to me. I miss you. I love you, and I want to get back on track."

"No," I said again. "You can't make me!" At that point, I knew that I had won. I knew I was going to stay home like I wanted. Dad was too upset to yell at me or force me to do anything.

"Ok," Dad tried again. "How about we just talk on the phone for a little bit? Let's catch up now. How are you? How's school?"

"Why do you care?" I shouted.

"Because I love you."

"No, you don't!" I screamed. "Just leave me alone!" I hung up the phone and ran to my room.

I was crying again, and I was mad at the same time. I could've talked to him on the phone, but I didn't want to. I didn't want to change my mind about seeing him. Mom needed me, and I wanted to stay home and have another special weekend with her. I wanted Danny to go away so there would be peace and quiet in the house. I also wanted to be mature and not cry. I felt stupid for missing my dad when I knew that we were better off without him.

He was stupid and lazy. Mom wanted to move on because he was no good and her friends supported her. Everyone said she was better off without him and that meant that I was too.

***

There was no slumber party that night, but I did hear Mom on the phone with someone. She was talking about me and my dad.

"She absolutely refused."

"Haha, the trashcan! That's so true!" she laughed a little, and I figured she was talking about my dad's apartment.

"Well, she knows what's up. She can see it."

"I think she lost her respect for him. This process brings out peoples' true colors, you know?"

"No, she told him herself. He can't blame me this time. It's her decision."

"I know. I wish he would wake up and realize what he's done. I don't blame her at all for the way she feels, and I completely support her decision."

I wasn't sure who she was talking to. I didn't think it was my aunt. Perhaps it was someone from the party or maybe even someone from work. Mom seemed to have a lot more people to talk to since my dad moved out.

I was happy to know that Mom supported me. She even seemed proud of me for being able to see the truth about my dad and stand up to him. I was proud of myself too. I'd grown a lot since my parents separated. I could see things differently, and Mom was treating me like I was more than just her kid. It felt good.

***

The next day my dad called. He asked to speak to me first, but I told Mom I didn't want to talk to him. She relayed the message, which started a fight.

"I asked her, and she doesn't want to speak to you."

"I think she's old enough to make that decision."

"No. And where is Danny anyway? Are you even watching him?"

"And you can see him?"

"Well, excuse me. It's a little nerve-wracking considering the fact that you once lost Gina in a department store."

"I think it is. We're talking about the safety of my children. You have a history that makes me nervous!"

"I told you, she doesn't want to talk to you."

"You heard her last night. It's not my fault. I'm not forcing her."

"Maybe you should apologize to her for what you've done."

"No, she doesn't. Perhaps you could send her an email or write a letter."

"No, I won't."

"You know, it's not my fault that you don't pay enough support to keep the house. It's not my fault that you moved out and started dating some immature bimbo. It's not my fault that you aren't helping to pay the college expenses of her brother. Your actions have shown nothing but your self-centered arrogance. She sees this stuff. She knows!"

"Why? I think she's made some pretty accurate conclusions. You want me to tell her she's mistaken? That she can't trust her own senses?!

Oh, yeah, that's a real good solution."

"You sound just like your mother. You think everything is so simple and everything has a happy ending and you *never* do *anything* wrong! I'm so sick of it! You left me here, in this house to care for our children while you went off doing God-knows what with God-knows-who. You're barely supporting us. And everyone knows it. Everyone knows that you abandoned your family for your own selfish reasons. What kind of man does that? And now you're glimpsing the consequences, and you're surprised? Give me a break! What did you expect? You think she should still want to be your little girl after what you've done to her?"

"YES, YOU DID!"

"How dare you say that to me when I'm the one who's here right now?"

"Your whole family is like that, every single one of them! You all think you're perfect, and you piss on the rest of the world. Remember what your father told you when we started dating?"

"But that doesn't just go away! And where are your parents now, huh? Why aren't they calling here for the kids? Why aren't they sending them letters and back-to-school care packages?"

"Well, that hardly benefits Gina. It doesn't show any respect for her at all. Could they be any less considerate?"

"I wouldn't bank on it at this point."

"NO, IT'S NOT!"

"Oh, no you won't!"

"ABSOLUTELY NOT! And I am not going to discuss this with you any further. You've done enough damage already!"

I assumed that Mom hung up the phone because she let out a big scream and then stomped outside to the patio. Slowly, I opened my bedroom door and tiptoed across the hallway to the bathroom so I could check on her. She was sitting in a chair with her elbows propped on the table and her face in her hands. I couldn't tell if she was crying, but I knew she wanted to be alone.

I was seething inside. I didn't know why my dad called to fight with her and ruin our quiet weekend. I didn't understand why he couldn't leave me alone like I told him to. It wasn't fair for him to put Mom in the middle and stress her out. It wasn't her fault. I wanted to know how he lost me in a department store, and I was curious about what Grandpa had said about my mom before my parents got married. I was pretty sure it had something to do with the fact that Mom had Kevin and had never been married to his dad.

For years, I listened to my mom say mean things about my dad's parents. I hadn't paid much attention because my parents always said nasty things when they were fighting and then they would make up and everything would be OK again. Since the separation, there was no making up and pretending things were alright. Since the separation, the insults were final, and they were beginning to add up.

I started to realize that my dad's parents were a little snobby. They always took expensive vacations, and they drove luxury cars. Grandma liked to buy me designer clothes, probably because she thought my other clothes weren't up to her standards. I remembered that when I started middle school, they offered to pay for private school instead. I guessed my school wasn't good enough for them either. Mom was right about Dad's family. How could I not have seen it?

Chapter 5: October

One night after dinner, Dad called and spoke briefly to Mom. She took the phone outside so I couldn't hear what they were saying. She didn't talk long, and then she came inside and handed the phone to Danny.

"Hi," Danny said.

"Cool!"

"OK!"

He was nodding his head excitedly, and then he took the phone from his ear and tried to hand it to me. I shook my head, walked down the hall to my bedroom, and shut the door.

When Danny knocked on my door a few minutes later, I let him in. He was smiling and jumping around.

"Daddy rented a cabin at the lake," he said.

I shrugged. "I'm sure his girlfriend will enjoy that," I told him.

Danny looked puzzled for a second. "Daddy doesn't have a girlfriend," he said and then laughed. "It's for us, silly! Next time we go with Daddy we have a three-day weekend. And Daddy wants to take us to the lake! We're going to have a campfire and go hiking!"

"Well, have fun," I told him. I grabbed Danny's shoulders, turned him around, and pushed him toward the door. "Now go play. I have homework to do."

Danny exited obediently, and I sat on my bed. I wasn't doing a very good job of keeping Danny out of Mom's way. It seemed like I was always too busy or too irritable to deal with him as much as I used to. I felt bad because I knew he would go and bother Mom, but I really wanted to be alone.

I thought about the last time we went to the lake. It was two years ago. We rented a cabin called "The Bear's Den." We spent a lot of time hiking and fishing. I taught Danny how to catch salamanders. One night Mom insisted upon cooking a standard dinner in the kitchen instead of having hot dogs on the campfire. We sat outside on the porch to eat, and when I was sure she wasn't watching, I used a spoon to fling my peas far into the woods. At one point, Dad saw me, and I felt my face get hot. I thought I'd be in trouble, but he smiled, winked and flung a pea off his own plate.

I did want to go to the lake again. I wanted to get away from everything and be on vacation. Thinking about the last trip made me miss my dad. I missed his jokes and the way he was always up for a new adventure. I missed the way he used to help me with my homework. I felt like calling him just to chat and catch up.

But I couldn't. I knew that I was just grieving the way Mom did at first. The great guy I thought was my dad never actually existed, and now he was trying to bribe me with a vacation because he wanted me to forget that he was a jerk. I was smarter than that, and I wouldn't let him fool me.

I choked back tears and called Sarah. I told her that I needed a break from my family and asked if I could spend the upcoming long weekend with her. She checked

77

with her mom and confirmed that it would be OK. I knew I could count on her. She felt sorry for me and my situation.

***

While I was at Sarah's house, I felt like I was under a microscope. It was obvious that Sarah's mom was concerned about me. She kept asking if I'd had enough to eat, if I was comfortable or if she could do anything for me. She even went out of her way to make pancakes for me each morning while Sarah and her dad ate cereal and bagels. It was nice to have someone cater to me, yet at the same time I felt like I was being treated like a toddler.

Sarah's parents had a good relationship. They'd been married for more than fifteen years, and they didn't fight at all. When they disagreed, they talked about it until they laughed. In that way, Sarah was lucky. She didn't have to deal with the same drama that I did. Her life at home was happy and comfortable.

Even though her home life was more comfortable than mine, I wasn't too envious. Sarah seemed younger to me. She didn't know anything about college or contracts or mortgages. She didn't know how much things cost. She never thought twice before asking her parents to buy something she wanted. Their house was always a little on the messy side, so she didn't worry about keeping things clean. And Sarah was an only child, which meant she wasn't responsible for looking after anyone else on a regular basis.

I should've felt carefree at Sarah's house, but instead I was bored and sad. Sometimes I was even annoyed with Sarah. I wondered how my mom was doing and if she was lonely. I felt guilty for not being home to help her get ready for the move. I knew she'd find lots of old memories in the basement and she might be upset. I worried about Danny at the lake with my dad. I hoped Dad was keeping an eye on him. I spent a lot of time counting the hours until I could go home.

***

I timed my homecoming so I'd get back after Danny. I didn't want to run into my dad and I missed him by just a few minutes. Danny was still talking excitedly about his weekend when I walked in the door.

"And I got to sleep on the top bunk!" he exclaimed.

Mom nodded politely. I could tell by the look on her face that she was tired and didn't feel like hearing Danny talk about the great time he had with Dad.

"Did Daddy bring a railing so you wouldn't fall off?" she asked him.

Danny looked confused and shook his head. "I didn't fall off," he told her.

Mom shook her head and looked away. She wasn't happy that my father had put Danny in danger by letting him sleep so high off the ground without a railing.

I decided to interrupt and save Mom. "Danny, why don't you meet me in the laundry room? You can tell me all about the lake while I put my dirty clothes in the washer."

Mom looked at me and mouthed "thank you." I knew the drill: Danny was usually super happy when he came back from Dad's. Mom was usually happy to see him but not happy to hear about his weekend. It was my job to make them both more comfortable. I was getting pretty good at it.

***

Two weeks later it was time to move. Conveniently, this provided me with another excuse not to see my dad. I sent him a text message to let him know I wouldn't be seeing him again, and he wrote back, "OK. I miss you."

When Dad came to pick up Danny, Mom met him outside to let him know where the new house was so he could take Danny there on Sunday. I was sitting on the front porch with a book, and I could hear the discussion even though they didn't realize it. Dad asked about me and when he would see me again.

"This is a big change for her. She's under a lot of stress," Mom told him.

"Well, I don't want to let things go much longer," Dad said. "I realize she's almost a teenager, and she's dealing with a lot of difficult issues. People told me to be patient. Everyone said she'd come around. Under normal circumstances, perhaps she would. But in this case, with the separation, the distance between us keeps growing."

"I think she needs more time," Mom said.

"We'll see about that," Dad stepped to the side and looked at me. I quickly looked down at my book.

"I love you, Gina!" Dad called before turning back to his car where Danny was waiting.

***

It took a long time to move everything to the new house. By Sunday night, Mom and I were exhausted.

When Danny arrived, he swept into the house like a tornado. He was hyper and thundered up the stairs to his room. I heard him rummaging around, and then he began asking questions.

"Where are my robots? Where are my army men? How did my Tower of Doom get broken?"

Mom was in the living room sorting through boxes of pictures and other decorations. She was shaking her head and muttering to herself about how the world wasn't going to end because the robots were missing.

I walked up the stairs and down the hall to Danny's room. I explained that there were still a lot of boxes in the basement and that some of our things got a little banged around while they were being transported. He seemed to understand, and he asked me to help him find and unpack more of his toys.

"Not tonight," I told him. "Mom and I are super tired from working all weekend. It was really hectic around here."

Danny frowned.

"How was your weekend?" I asked, not really wanting to hear the answer.

"It was good. And ... sad. But good!" Danny said. "Me and Daddy went to a museum, and we went hiking, and we played checkers. And we talked about the old house."

"What did you say about the old house?" I wanted to know.

Danny shrugged. "We talked about how much we would miss it. Daddy was sad too. He told me about when you moved in and ate spaghetti at the picnic table."

I remembered our first night in the old house. We did eat spaghetti at the picnic table, which was set up in the dining room because we didn't have a dining room table yet. That first night, I slept in my room, but there were no sheets on my mattress because Mom didn't have time to find them before I went to bed. I slept under my old pink and yellow comforter.

I smiled. "Yeah, I remember that too."

"Um, Gina?" Danny asked.

"What?"

81

"Um ... . Is Mommy mad at me?"

"What? No. She's just worn out from moving all weekend. It was a lot of hard work," I told him.

"Not just today," he said. "I don't think she likes me when I come back from Daddy's."

I knew what he was talking about. But he was wrong. It wasn't that Mom didn't like him. It was that Mom didn't like Dad. Danny just didn't get it.

"Mom likes you," I told him. "She just needs space sometimes. Remember when Dad told you that sometimes she has bad days?"

Danny nodded.

"Well, Sunday nights are a busy time. Mom has a lot of work to do on Sundays, especially tonight because so much of our stuff is still in boxes."

Danny looked down. "OK," he said.

I wasn't convinced he felt better. I didn't know what else to do. I wanted to explain things to Danny, but I didn't think he would understand. And I didn't want him to tell Dad and start another fight between our parents. Now that we were in the new house, I was hoping for a fresh start.

Chapter 6: November

As soon as Halloween was over, people began talking about Christmas. Decorations went up around town, at school, and at the mall. I started craving my mom's pumpkin pie and humming holiday music in the shower. I don't know why I was surprised when Dad called to talk about a special custody schedule for the holidays.

We'd enjoyed a delicious dinner and were working together to clean up the kitchen. Everyone was in a good mood at our new house. It was starting to feel like home— like a new, happier home. Then Mom's phone rang.

I could tell by the face she made before she answered that it was my dad.

"Hello," she said.

"I figured this was coming," she said as she moved from the kitchen to the living room. "What did you have in mind?"

"Thank you, that's very considerate."

"That whole weekend? No, I didn't have anything special planned."

"Travel? Do you think that's a good idea?"

"No, actually I don't."

"You know how she's been. That's going to be way too much to ask of her."

"I don't know. What do you want me to do?"

"That's not my fault!"

"You want me to lie to her? Do you think she's stupid?"

"Obviously you do."

"I'm not saying that. My point is that she hasn't wanted to see you at all. Not at my house or your apartment or the lake. I don't think it's a good idea for you to drag her out of town for four days given the history. What if she runs away? What will you do then?"

"She hasn't seen them or talked to them either!"

"Yes, I can."

"NO!"

"Why? You don't believe me?"

"Oh, fine. Hold on, let me find her."

Mom came walking into the kitchen with the phone in her hand. She held it out to me. "It's Doug," she said flatly. "He wants to speak to you."

For a second I wasn't sure who "Doug" was, even though I knew she'd been talking to my dad. I hesitated as I took the phone from her.

"Hello?" I said.

"Hi, Honey, it's Dad," my dad said.

"I know," I told him.

"Listen, I was just talking to your mom about Thanksgiving and the weekend after. I'm going to go to Grandma and Grandpa's house. Danny's going to come with me, and we'd love for you to come along too. The whole family will be there, and they miss you."

My heart sank. I missed Dad's family, but now that I knew the truth, I didn't want to see them. My grandparents were snobs and probably only wanted to see me so they could make judgments about my mom. I also didn't want to spend so much time in the car with my dad. Plus, Mom already told him that I wouldn't want to go. I couldn't disappoint her after she'd been so proud of me for taking her side.

"I don't want to," I told him.

"Honey, I think this will be a good thing, don't you? We'll have lots of time in the car to catch up, and you'll be able to see Laurie and the rest of your family. We'll have a good time."

I was sad. I didn't want to blow off everyone, but I felt like I didn't have a choice. If I agreed, Mom would feel like I crossed her, and Dad would feel like he won. I thought for a second and then took Mom's cue in calling my dad by his first name. It was easier to stand up to him if I didn't think of him as my dad.

"That's your family, Doug," I stated firmly. "My family is here."

There was silence on the other end of the phone. I held my breath.

Finally, he spoke. "Gina, we're all a family. It doesn't matter how often you see your family members. They're still there. And they love you. *We* love you, and we miss you."

"That's nice, but you don't have to do that." I told him, reminding myself that I was talking to "Doug" and not "Dad."

"No," he said. "I want to. You're my daughter, and I want to be a part of your life. I want you to be part of my life."

"No, really, it's OK," I began. "I'm better off now that you're not around. Our house is happier, and nobody trips over your stuff. We don't have to worry about your parents coming to inspect how we live. And as long as you don't call or come over, there's no fighting either. I wish you would stay away forever!"

I spun around and handed the phone to my mom, who was staring at me with wide eyes. She took it from me, took a deep breath, and brought it to her ear.

"Stop, Doug. She doesn't want to talk to you anymore."

"What do you want me to do? She's her own person."

"That would be abusive. She's practically a teenager."

"No, I don't. I think she'd run away ... or at the very least, she'd cause a scene."

"She's determined. She made up her mind, and she told you so herself."

"Don't blame me. This is her decision."

"No, she's not. She's intelligent and responsible. She's not a child, like Danny, and she deserves to exercise some independence."

"Well, sometimes things don't go according to plan."

"I don't think that's a good idea. I certainly don't want to share any space with you right now. I despise you!"

"Don't you get it? She doesn't want to see you! Why should I upset her like that?"

"That's because she's realized that you're not Mr. Wonderful. And that's the truth."

"For what? She's doing fine. She's working hard in school. She has friends. Her friends haven't changed. She's not experimenting with drugs. She doesn't have a boyfriend. Everything is fine! The only problem is you!"

"What do you mean?"

"Why?"

"She's a smart girl. There's nothing wrong with that."

"Do you think I can't handle this? What, like I'm an unfit mother?"

"But I didn't do anything!"

"THAT'S NOT MY FAULT!"

"NO, YOU WILL NOT!"

"There is nothing wrong with her! And there's nothing wrong with me. I'm a good parent. I take care of my kids, which is more than can be said for you. Stop blaming me for the fallout of what you've done. You're the one who is absent. You're the one who chose to be a bachelor instead of a father. You're the one she hates!"

"Did you hear me? She *hates* you. You've caused nothing but anguish for her lately. Stop making this about you and start having some consideration for your daughter."

"Of course I do."

"Maybe you should have thought about that before you decided you wanted a divorce. Now you're getting what you wanted, aren't you? And we are fine. We're going to be just fine as long as you stop trying to butt in and cause problems. I don't need a doctor to tell me that much!"

"That will never, ever happen. Do you understand me? You will NOT take my children away!"

I wondered if the people on the other side of the wall could hear Mom screaming. In my room, I was crying into my pillow. I felt horrible. Dad— Doug— was mad at my mom because of how I felt. He was blaming her. I tried to do what she wanted, what I knew was best, and it started another fight between them anyway. A really big fight. It sounded like he was saying she was a bad mother and she shouldn't have custody of us. Things kept getting worse!

Before too long, Mom came into my room and sat on my bed. She reached out and picked me up as best she could, and she held me while I cried. She was crying too.

"I'm sorry!" I wailed. "I'm so sorry."

"For what?" Mom asked.

"For everything! All I did was tell him how I felt, just like you always told me to do! And he got mad at you and put you in the middle and—" I broke off into sobs.

"Shhh," Mom was holding me tight and rocking me. "It's not your fault. None of this is your fault. I'm sorry he made you feel that way. That's just one of the mind games he plays. It's OK. Everything is going to be OK."

"What did he say?" I asked. "Does he want to get custody of me and Danny?"

Mom shook her head dismissively. "He said a lot of things. He talked about doctors and lawyers and judges ... But don't worry, I won't let anyone take you away from me."

I didn't understand what Doug might be planning. I hated him. Mom was right about that. I hated him with everything I had. He'd left and ruined my life. He was always fighting with my mom. He was irresponsible with my brother. He didn't respect my feelings. His family was stuck up and they'd taught him to be self-centered. And he was going to try and take me away from my mom. My mother! The person who took care of me. She was the only person I could count on, and he wanted to take me away from her.

"What's going to happen?" I asked.

"I don't know," Mom said. "But I promise, no matter what, I won't let anything happen to you. If we have to go to court, just tell the judge the truth and don't be afraid."

Court? I didn't want to go to court! I didn't want to sit at the front of one of those big rooms like I saw on TV and talk to a judge while everyone stared at me. I started to wonder when that would be and how long it would take. I was sure I'd have to take time off school and then everyone would know what was going on. That would be embarrassing! It was yet another way for Doug to mess things up for me.

"When will that happen?" I wanted to know.

Mom shook her head as she answered, "I have no idea, Hon. I think that's something the lawyers work out."

"Mom, is this better?" I asked.

"Better than what, Sweetie?"

"Better than before. When we all still lived together and you would fight a lot, but then you'd make up." I started to whimper again.

"That's a good question," she said, rubbing my back. "Sometimes, I don't know."

***

The next week there was a science fair at school. Jenny, Sarah and I entered a project together and won an Honorable Mention for showing the differences in effectiveness between natural and chemical cleaning products. After school was over, there was an open exhibit for the public to come in and look at the students' work. Of course, Mom and Danny came.

It was an exciting night. The cafeteria was full of people who complimented us on our display. After an hour of answering questions, Sarah and I took a bathroom break and left Jenny at our booth for a few minutes.

Sarah and I fixed our hair at the mirror and then walked out of the bathroom, laughing and talking. We turned the corner to the hallway leading back to the cafeteria, and that was when I saw him: Doug. He'd just walked in the front door and was looking around. My heart jumped into my throat, and I stopped in my tracks. Just then, he looked my way, and we made eye contact.

I turned quickly and walked the other way, thinking I would take a longer route to the cafeteria. Then he started to follow me. I walked faster, but I could hear him behind me. He was getting closer, and he was calling out to me.

"Gina, wait!"

I felt nervous. I didn't know why he was there. I remembered Mom saying he wanted to take me away from her. What if he was there to kidnap me?

I panicked. My heart was thudding in my ears, and I started to cry. I broke out into a run and took off as fast as I could and ran past the bathrooms. The hallway was empty and I could hear his footsteps echoing behind me.

"Leave me alone!" I screamed as I darted past the trophy case.

I kept going, full speed, until I reached the cafeteria. I looked around and saw Mom standing beside a display of rocks with Danny. I ran to her, sobbing, and threw my arms around her.

Doug showed up a second behind me, just as Mom was asking what had happened. When she saw him, her voice took a different tone.

"What's going on?" she asked. "What did you do to her?"

"N— nothing," he stammered. "I wanted to say hello, and she ran away. I didn't do anything."

I refused to look at him. I kept my face buried in Mom's shoulder. I was still crying and clinging to her. By that time, the people around us had grown quiet. I could feel their eyes on me.

"I think you've done enough damage tonight," my mom told Doug. "You should go now."

He reached out and touched my shoulder with the tips of his fingers. I felt a jolt and heard a slapping sound as Mom forced him to retreat. "Don't you see what you've done to her?" she asked, holding me a little tighter.

Then I heard the voice of Mr. Roebuck, our principal. "Is there a problem?" he asked.

I loosened my grip on Mom and looked down. My hair was clinging to my cheeks, and my nose was running. I was a mess. I glanced at Doug. He looked confused.

He shook his head. "No, sir," he said to Mr. Roebuck. "I apologize. I was just leaving."

Mr. Roebuck looked at my mom, and she nodded her head to let him know we were OK. Danny let out a yelp and ran after Doug, who paused just briefly to kneel down and talk to my brother.

When Danny came back, he kicked me in the ankle. "Why'd you do that?" he asked. "You made Daddy sad!"

Mom put her arm around me again. "Danny, stop," she scolded. "I think it's time for us to go home."

Jenny and Sarah were concerned when I told them I was leaving. Sarah looked especially worried because she'd been there for the whole thing.

"What did your dad do?" she asked.

"It's a long story," I shook my head. "I'll see you guys tomorrow, OK?"

Back at home, Mom drew me a bubble bath and then made some hot tea.

"I'm sorry your dad ruined your night," she said as we sat in the kitchen. "I don't know what he was doing there. I certainly didn't tell him about the event."

"I know it's not your fault," I told her. "I got freaked out when I saw him. I thought he was going to steal me."

Mom sat back in her chair. "Steal you?"

I nodded. "You said he wanted to take me away from you. I got scared."

"Oh, Honey," she said, getting up from her seat. "You poor thing. That must've been horrible!" She put her hand on my shoulder and kissed the top of my head.

Suddenly, I felt ridiculous. "I'm sorry," I mumbled.

"Oh, no," she said thoughtfully. "I hadn't considered that at all. I suppose I don't really know what he would do. You were right to be cautious."

I still felt stupid. Even if it was OK to be careful around Doug, I'd made a big scene at school. My teachers and my friends saw it, and everyone would ask me a lot of questions the following day.

"He shouldn't have come," Mom said. "It was wrong of him to show up uninvited and scare you like that. Hopefully he's learned his lesson, especially after your principal had to intervene. Your dad didn't make a very favorable impression tonight."

"What should I tell people?" I asked.

"Tell them you're OK and you don't want to talk about it," she suggested.

I shrugged.

Mom stood up. "I'm going to bed," she announced. "Don't stay up too late, OK? You need your rest."

I nodded and took a deep breath. It had been a long night.

***

A few days later I went to Sarah's house after school and came home late. Mom had sent me a text message to tell me that she was taking Danny grocery shopping and we'd be having a delayed dinner. I wasn't surprised to find the house empty when I walked in. I decided to clean up the kitchen so we could start cooking as soon as Mom got back.

There was a pile of papers on the table and when I picked them up, I noticed that some of them were from my mom's lawyer. I paused and took a closer look. There were copies of letters that went back and forth between the attorneys, a few copies of checks, and a very official-looking document that talked about custody evaluations. Dad's lawyer was requesting an evaluation to see who Danny and I should live with!

I sat down at the table and looked closer. The paperwork contained a list of doctors and procedures and prices. And the prices were high. The letter from Doug's lawyer accused my mom of "withholding visitation" and "engaging in hostile communication." The letter from my mom's lawyer simply stated that he had received paperwork regarding a voluntary evaluation and that my mom should call him to discuss the details. He also enclosed an invoice stating that my mom owed him $876.32. I didn't understand why she owed so much money. The invoice only said that he had read her emails, returned her phone calls, and reviewed her file.

I was disgusted as I gathered the papers in a pile with the rest of the mail and moved them to Mom's basket on the counter. Doug was trying to make my mom look bad in front of the lawyers! He was trying to say that she was a bad mother, and he wanted to pay some professionals a lot of money to agree with him. The papers didn't say anything about court. I still didn't understand how any of it would work, but I knew I didn't like it. My stomach felt queasy. I didn't want to think about it anymore, so I opened my algebra book and started my homework instead.

I ate only half of my dinner that night. When Mom asked me if anything was wrong, I told her I wasn't hungry because I ate ice cream at Sarah's house. She didn't ask any more questions.

After dinner, I cleaned the kitchen with Danny and then checked on him while he got ready for bed. I wanted to make sure that he properly washed his hair and brushed his teeth, just in case I needed to tell a doctor or a judge.

After Danny and I were both in bed, I heard Mom on the phone with Aunt Tamara. She was talking about the papers she'd received from her lawyer.

"It's financial abuse! Not only is he threatening to take my kids away, he's making sure I have to give up a lot of money to fight him over it. He can just get more money from his parents, I'm sure of it. What does he care? It's all just a game to him!"

"Another nine hundred dollars! After I just paid off the ten thousand dollar bill when I sold the house. I don't know how much more of this I can take."

"Yes, I called Gill. He wasn't available as usual, so I left a message."

"Why would I do that?"

"I suppose you're right. I hadn't thought of that."

"Between ourselves? You want me to talk to him? I can't do that! Especially not now after what he's done."

"Do you realize that Gina is *afraid* of him? She is terrified. She knows he's careless and selfish, and he wants to take my children from me. This is her home, and he wants to take her out of it and force her to live in his trashcan! Can you imagine?"

"I have to support her. I'm all she has right now. We're the only ones who really get it."

"Sometimes I do. But it doesn't seem to bother her. She can handle anything."

"That would cost a lot of money too."

"No, I definitely don't want to ask Mom and Dad for help. Things are better now that the debt is reduced and my mortgage payment is lower. I'm sure it'll be fine."

"Yes, I'm sure."

"Thank you. I know."

"Maybe I'll call him and ask what he's thinking."

"Well, at least it won't cost me four hundred dollars."

"OK."

"Yes, I will."

"Goodnight."

I laid there, wide awake, in the darkness. I wanted to march downstairs and ask Mom what was going on, but I was afraid she'd just send me back to bed. She had talked about financial abuse and said it was all a game. Doug was doing everything just to hurt her— to hurt *us*! The more I thought about it, the more I started to like the idea of going to court. If I told the judge the truth about what Doug was doing, maybe he would go to jail and I wouldn't have to worry about him anymore. Then we could all get on with our lives. Danny would be sad, but it wouldn't last long after he heard the truth.

Everything would be so much better if Doug would just disappear.

***

As planned, Danny went with Doug for Thanksgiving. They left on Wednesday night and shortly after they drove away, Mom and I traveled to the bus station to pick up Kevin. He had a break from school, so he was coming home for the long weekend. I couldn't wait to see him.

Kevin looked the same when he got off the bus, except that his hair was a little longer. He was smiling as he gave us each a hug, and then he handed Mom a bunch of wilted flowers.

"Sorry," he told her. "They didn't travel well."

Mom was so happy that she got a little teary. She offered to take Kevin to dinner anywhere he wanted to go. But Kevin was tired and said he only wanted to go home. He was eager to see the new house.

During the ride in the car, Kevin talked a lot about his new girlfriend, Ginny.

"She was named after Virginia Woolf," he told Mom. "Her parents are both English teachers."

Mom nodded politely. I could tell she wanted to hear more about Kevin and less about Kevin's girlfriend, but she didn't say anything.

Kevin went on, "She's really great. I'd like you to meet her over the winter break. We talked about going to each other's houses. She lives about an hour and a half from here."

"I'd like that," Mom said. "Now, tell me about school. How is that history class going? The last I heard from you, the professor was a bear and you thought you were destined to fail."

"I got a B on my latest paper," he told her. "So I think I might pass after all. And my other instructors are pretty cool. College is so much better than high school!"

At home, we took Kevin on a tour of the house and showed him the room where he would be sleeping. He was positive and polite about all of it. He didn't even complain that most of his stuff was in boxes in the basement. We ordered a pizza and played video games until it got late, and then Mom went to bed.

After she'd been gone for a few minutes, Kevin turned to me. "So, I hear things aren't so great with you and your dad," he said.

I shrugged. "Divorce brings out people's true colors, I guess."

"You know," Kevin lowered his voice to make sure Mom wouldn't hear him from upstairs. "I still talk to your dad. And I still think he's a good guy. I know he really misses you."

I wondered how much Kevin had talked to Doug. And I wondered how much they talked about me. But I was afraid that Doug had asked Kevin to talk to me about him, so I didn't want to give Kevin any information. However, I wanted to *get* information.

"I guess that means he's still giving you money," I concluded, staring at the TV.

Kevin laughed a little. "Yeah, he is. We talk on a regular basis, and I let him know what I need. He gets it to me real quick."

"I guess it's good that he's taking care of someone in this family," I said icily.

"C'mon, Gina. He takes care of everyone in this family. Even if you won't see him, he still supports you by giving Mom money to pay for the things you need."

"Yeah," I said sarcastically, gesturing to our surroundings. "He's taking care of us real well."

Kevin sighed and shook his head. "You're probably just too young to understand," he said.

That made me angry. How dare he say that I was too young to understand? I understood everything. Mom was always telling people how mature I was when it came to their situation. Kevin didn't know what he was talking about because he wasn't there. He didn't see what a lazy and irresponsible person Doug was. He didn't know about the financial abuse and custody evaluations. Kevin was just like I was a few months before. He was the one who didn't get it.

I tossed my game controller and stood up. "It's hard to believe they let you into college," I told him. Then I turned and went upstairs to bed.

***

For the rest of the weekend, Kevin and I acted as if nothing had happened. We ate Thanksgiving dinner at Aunt Tamara's house. Some of Kevin's friends came over on Friday, and Saturday he and his friends went out. I spent a lot of time communicating with Jenny and Sarah. Saturday, we met at Jenny's house to watch movies. Sunday, Doug brought Danny home early so he could spend some time with Kevin before we took him to the bus station.

Overall, it was a good vacation. Aside from that one conversation, there was no more talk about Doug. Nobody said anything at all about the custody evaluations. We had a nice time. Kevin said he would be back in a few weeks and then he'd be home for almost a month. And that was when he'd bring Ginny home to meet us. I looked forward to it.

Chapter 7: December

After Thanksgiving, I started getting text messages from Doug on a regular basis. They usually came daily and contained a single sentence.

My heart is broken.
You were born on a Wednesday.
I'm wearing the tie you gave me for my birthday.
What did I do?
How was school?

I got used to them quickly and was able to ignore them. I never sent a response, and I didn't bother telling Mom about them because I didn't want to upset her. One day he sent one that struck a nerve and left me feeling broken:

Remember when you rode on the four-wheeler?

I got the message while I was making a peanut butter sandwich in the kitchen. At first all I could do was stare at my phone. I *did* remember ...

It was the day before my fifth birthday, and the mailman brought a package for me. I was excited and begged my parents to let me open it early.

Dad told me that I could open it under one condition: that I go for a ride on a four-wheeler with him. He'd wanted me to come along since he started riding the trails at his friend's house. Until that point, I'd been too scared. I didn't like the noise, and I was afraid I'd fall off. But the temptation of an early birthday present changed my mind. I told him I'd do it.

I ended up having a great time riding the trail with my dad. He sat me firmly in front of him and reached his arms around me to hold the handlebars. I got used to the noise, and he didn't go too fast. Out in the woods, I felt free with the wind blowing through my hair and the smell of summer all around me. I started riding with Dad on a regular basis until we moved to our house and were too far away.

In the kitchen, I shoved my phone into my pocket and tried to forget about it. That was a long time ago. It was no use to think about the past.

I managed to hold back the memory until about halfway through dinner. I was forcing a fat spaghetti sandwich into my mouth when Mom mentioned a holiday toy drive at her office.

"They're collecting all kinds of toys, even if they've been used," she told us. "So I was thinking that after we eat, the two of you could go through some of those boxes in the basement and pick out things to donate. It's a good way for us to clear up some more space in the house."

Danny looked curious. "Will they give them back?" he asked.

Mom shook her head. "No, Hon. When you donate something, it means that you're giving it away so that someone else can have it. The toys will go to kids who don't have toys of their own. You'll want to make sure that you choose things that you know you won't want to play with again. For example, I was thinking that maybe Gina would want to donate her Blue-Eyed Doll collection."

That was what did it. The present I so desperately wanted to open more than seven years earlier had been the very first doll in my Blue-Eyed Doll collection. The memory of Dad hit me hard— again. Suddenly, I couldn't eat anymore. I put down my sandwich, looked at my hands, and started to cry.

"Gina?" Mom asked. "Gina, what's wrong? You don't have to donate your dolls. I just thought it was a nice idea."

I shook my head. I opened my mouth, but I couldn't form any words. I didn't know what to say.

Mom got up from her seat and rushed to my side. She put her hands on my shoulders and led me to stand up and walk out of the kitchen.

"Danny, finish your dinner," she called as we moved to the living room where we sat down on the couch.

I grabbed a pillow after I sat down and tried to think of a way to explain myself. Mom looked startled and concerned. She reached for my hand and begged me to tell her what was wrong.

"Dad—" I began, and had to pause to catch my breath. "Dad ... has been sending me text messages ..." I stopped again to breathe, and Mom flew into a rage.

"He WHAT?" she demanded to know. "What has he been saying to you?"

I shook my head. "Nothing really," I told her. "It's just ... the one he sent today ..."

"Let me see," she said, holding out her hand.

I handed her my phone, and she clicked away as she read through the messages he'd sent. She looked at me, her face softening for a moment.

"Oh, Honey, I'm so sorry," she said, her voice almost a whisper. "I wish you had told me about this before. Why don't you go upstairs and get cleaned up? I'm going to put a stop to this now."

She gave me a hug and patted my shoulder as I stood up. I started to cry harder. It was too much. I hadn't told Mom about the messages because I didn't want her to get mad. Then Doug had to send that one to make me remember our happy times ... now Mom was mad because I hadn't told her earlier. And she'd yell at Doug, and he'd be mad at her again. I felt sad and angry and guilty and ashamed and lonely and confused. I plodded up to my room and fell onto my bed.

Downstairs, I could hear Mom on the phone.

"Doug, she hates you! She is terrified of you! Please, stop."

"No, you're not. You are harassing another person."

"Well, she's certainly old enough to decide she wants nothing to do with you. Why can't you show her some respect?"

"Oh, WHY do you have to make everything so damn complicated? Just leave her alone!"

"A restraining order? Well, maybe I will. I've already prepared her to take the stand against you in court. If that's what we need to do, then that's what we'll do. But, is that what you want? Do you want your name drug through the mud all over town? Do you want everyone to know that the law had to step in to protect your daughter from you? Are you sure?"

"What, are you crying now? My God, Doug. Can't you handle anything like an adult?"

"It's your fault!"

"Yes, it is. She saw how you acted. She saw how you treated me and her brother, and she made a decision based on that. You've got nobody to blame but yourself."

"Quite the opposite. She is fine as long as you're not in the picture. The moment someone mentions your name, she changes."

"I told you, she is not ill!"

"No, it will cost way too much money … Money that I don't have."

"I'm sorry, Doug. I can't help you with this. I need to support my daughter because she is the one who is suffering because of you. If you can't give her what she needs, then I'll have to do whatever is necessary to protect her."

That was the last I heard of their conversation. Mom must've hung up the phone then because I heard her go into the kitchen and talk to Danny about the dishes.

I felt sick in my stomach. Mom was fuming. Dad was crying! They were talking about court and restraining orders. Mom thought she needed to protect me. I wondered why she wanted to protect me when she was always saying that I was so grown up ... and I thought I was the one protecting her! I wondered how it got to be that way. It wasn't that long ago that the five of us lived together and one of the House Rules was to respect other people. At the same time, it felt like that was an entire lifetime ago.

I felt like I needed to keep crying, but I didn't have any tears left. I was disappointed in myself for crying all the time. I was angry at Danny because he didn't have to deal with the things I did. I thought about running away. I imagined getting up the next morning and packing my backpack full of clothes, then walking out the door and, instead of going to the bus stop, I would just keep walking. I'd walk until I got too tired and then I'd stop and ... *and what?* I realized I couldn't rent a hotel room, and I didn't know anybody who would be willing to hide me from my family.

Just then I heard Mom on the stairs. A moment later she knocked on my door.

"What?" I asked.

She opened the door and poked her head in. "Honey, are you OK?"

"I'm fine," I said, staring at the wall.

"Do you want to talk?"

"No."

"Is there anything I can do for you?"

I laughed sarcastically. "Can you fix it? Can you turn back time?"

Mom was silent. Then quietly she said, "No, Honey. You know I can't do that."

"Then how about leaving me alone?" I asked. I sounded rude, and I knew it. I also didn't care. I wasn't in the mood to talk about it anymore. Another evening had been ruined by that stupid situation, and I was sick of it.

Mom opened the door and started across the room.

"Didn't you hear me?" I asked.

She stopped. "I just wanted—"

"I don't care!" I shouted. "I don't care what you wanted. Nobody seems to care what I wanted! I wanted to have a normal day and a normal night. I wanted to get my homework done without crying all over it. I wanted to stay in our old house. I wanted to have parents who didn't hate each other. Now I want you to leave me alone!"

Mom's eyes filled with tears and she turned away without another word. It didn't bother me. For months, I'd worried about her. I'd helped out and taken her side because she needed me. That night, I didn't want to think about her or Danny or anyone else. I just wanted to lie in the dark and forget who I was.

***

Kevin came home a few days before my winter break began. He started planning for his girlfriend's visit as soon as he got settled.

"Mom, I was thinking of having Ginny stay for the weekend," he said one night after dinner. "Then, I'll go visit her the next weekend, after Christmas."

Mom nodded from her position at the kitchen sink. "That's fine, Kevin. I hope this girl is as wonderful as you say she is. You know, you've really built her up in my mind."

Kevin smiled. "She's great, Mom. You'll see. And Gina," he turned to me. "I think the three of us should do something fun on Saturday. I think you'll like her a lot."

I was excited to meet Ginny, and I was glad that Kevin wanted me to hang out with the two of them. I liked the thought of getting out of the house and spending time with people who were older. I'd become bored with my friends in the recent months.

***

The following Saturday, Kevin, Ginny and I set out for lunch at a local coffee bar. I ordered a large hot chocolate and a grilled cheese sandwich. My brother and his girlfriend ordered fancy coffee drinks. We picked a comfy area in the corner and sat down to chat.

I don't know how we got on the subject of Doug and the divorce, but somehow we did. I didn't mind, though. Ginny had a lot of questions, and she was easy to talk to. Her parents were also divorced, and she seemed to understand a lot.

"You mean you don't see your dad at all?" she asked me.

I shook my head. "No," I told her.

"Don't you miss him?" she asked with a frown. "I used to miss my dad so much during the times we were apart."

I shook my head again. "My dad's a jerk," I said. "I want nothing to do with him."

"What did he do?" she wanted to know.

"He's just a bad father. He's selfish and irresponsible."

"Wow," Ginny said thoughtfully. "I guess you must've been happy about the separation, then. I mean, since you don't like him anyway."

"Actually," I began, straightening a little in my chair. "I didn't have any idea what he was like before the divorce. I used to think he was great. It's only been since the separation that I've been able to see what a loser he is. Like, how irresponsible he is with my brother and how little he cares about our family. The divorce has been a real eye-opening experience for me." I felt proud sitting there, talking to someone older about how much I'd grown up in the past six months.

Ginny took a sip of her fancy drink. "You mean your little brother still sees him? Even though your dad doesn't take care of him?"

I paused. I hadn't thought about it that way, exactly. For a second I wondered why Mom would let Danny stay with Doug, knowing that Danny wasn't safe with him. Then I remembered the lawyer's bill.

"Doug is financially abusing my mom," I told her. "He's making the divorce cost so much money that she can't afford to fight him. And Danny doesn't know any better. He's young and doesn't understand everything that's going on. He still wants to visit Doug."

"I see," Ginny nodded. "When my parents separated, my little sister was only four years old. She didn't understand either."

"One time my father came to my school science fair. He wasn't invited, and he caused a big scene. It was horrible. And Danny was so clueless, he ran after Doug even after the principal told him to leave."

Ginny looked at me sympathetically but didn't say anything.

I finished the last of my hot chocolate. When I raised my mug, Ginny commented on my bracelet, and we talked about jewelry until it was time to go.

I liked Ginny. She was fun and nice. And she was mature. I liked her sense of style, and we'd read a lot of the same books. After she left, I told Kevin that I thought she was a keeper. He tousled my hair and said he agreed.

***

A few days after Kevin returned from visiting Ginny's family, he dropped a bomb on us. We were in the living room. Mom was watching TV, and Danny was eating ice cream. I was toying with the new phone Mom bought me for Christmas. She also had my number changed, and I was double checking to make sure I'd updated everyone in my contact list. Everyone except Doug, of course. I'd gotten to "Jillian Jameson" when Kevin blurted it out.

"I think I'm going to call my real father," he said.

The room got very quiet. I couldn't even hear the TV anymore.

Mom's face turned white and then red. "What do you need to do that for?" she asked. "Is it about money?"

"No," Kevin shook his head. "I just want to talk to him. I want to meet him. I want to know where I came from and hear his story and understand ... " His voice trailed off.

Mom took a deep breath. "This isn't something we should discuss now," she said firmly. "Later."

After that, the atmosphere became very uncomfortable. We tried to lighten the mood by playing games and watching a funny show, but neither helped. A couple hours later, Danny went to bed, and I followed him. I didn't have to go to bed so early, but I didn't know what else to do.

Not long after I crawled under the covers, I heard the conversation in the living room.

"I just don't understand why. I've told you for years what an imbecile your father is. Why do you want to talk to him?" Mom sounded like she was on the verge of tears.

Unlike Mom, Kevin sounded confident. "Because I want to find out for myself. I don't remember anything about him, and I want to know. He created me, and all my life he's been missing. It feels weird."

"Oh, *you* feel weird? How do you think I feel right now? I've been with you since you were a baby. I changed your diapers and fed you and taught you to walk. I raised you to be the person you are. And now ... now you want ... *him*?"

"Mom, I just want to call the guy and talk to him."

"But why? After all this time?"

"I just told you!"

"He's not worthy of you!" Mom shouted.

"Ginny says—" Kevin started to offer, but Mom cut him off.

"Oh, is that what this is about? Did she put these thoughts in your head? You never spoke about him before now. What else did she tell you?"

"She said it's natural for me to want to meet my father. Children who were given up for adoption find their birth parents all the time. She said it's not odd that I wonder about him and if I got some answers, I'd feel better."

"I've given you the only answers you need. I raised you. Me. By myself. Not him. He doesn't deserve to know you."

"Mom, you weren't alone raising me. You had Doug."

"Yeah, and a fat lotta good that did us, huh? Where's he now?"

"There's nothing wrong with Doug. He's a good guy. It just didn't work out."

"Oh, is that what Ginny said too?"

"No. That's what I said. Ginny said Gina should see him."

"Oh boy, your little girlfriend is just full of wisdom, isn't she?"

"Well, she knows about this stuff. She studies it as part of her major."

"Right. Part of her major to butt into my life and corrupt my son against me?"

"Against you? No, Mom—" That was all he could get out before she interrupted him.

"Yes, against me. Look at you, standing here in my house, telling me what a bad job I've done!"

"I didn't say you did a bad job!"

"No, you said you want to find your father and that Gina should be with hers. What does that say about me?"

"It says kids should know both their parents!"

"You sound like the informational pamphlets in my attorney's office. Don't you think I know what's best for my kids? You turned out great. You're in college! And Gina is fine too. Sometimes one parent isn't … *stable* enough. And then it's up to the other parent to protect the children."

"Then why aren't you protecting Danny?"

"He's too young. He's just a little boy, and he doesn't understand!"

"All the more reason to protect him, right? Because he can't protect himself. But you don't. Every other weekend, you send him off to stay with his father, whom he loves. What's up with the double standard, Mom? Why can Danny love him, but Gina hates him? And she's like your trophy child because of it! Don't you think there's something wrong with that?"

"I DON'T HAVE TO ANSWER TO YOU!" Mom screamed. "Stop questioning me. I am your mother!"

"Right," I heard Kevin say. Then I heard heavy footsteps, the jingle of keys, and the slam of the door.

Lying in my bed, I felt cold and alone. I didn't know if I should be angry or sad. All I could think of were questions:

Where did Kevin go?
Was Mom OK?
Why did Ginny tell Kevin that I should see Doug?
What if Kevin found out that he had a sister on his father's side?
Was Mom doing something wrong?
Should everyone know their parents?
When would Danny be old enough to understand?
Why did Danny still love Dad?
Was Kevin right?
What was Ginny going to school for?
How did I feel about Doug?
How did I feel about Mom?
Was I really as mature as I thought I was?
Did I still want to be a part of the grown-up club?

I tossed and turned for hours before I finally fell asleep. Even then, I had horrible dreams about evil unicorns and scary old women with long fingernails.

Chapter 8: January

Kevin met his real father a few days before he was scheduled to go back to school. Mom wasn't happy about it, but Kevin told her there was nothing she could do to stop him. When he got back from the meeting, I was the only one home. I asked him how it went.

"It was good," he said. "I'm glad I did it."

"So, is your dad a loser?" I asked.

Kevin shook his head. "He's not. Actually, he has a wife and a son, and he's the head chef at an upscale restaurant."

When I heard that, I felt bad for Kevin. "Mom lied to you?"

He shook his head again. "Jake said that he was a lot younger when Mom had me. He wasn't ready to be a father, and he was scared. That's why he didn't fight when Mom said she wanted him out of our lives. He said he's regretted it ever since, but he's also glad that he didn't have the chance to screw up in front of me."

"OK, then. So he *was* a loser, but he's not anymore?"

Kevin shrugged. "No, I wouldn't say it like that. People mess up, Gina. Everyone makes mistakes, even parents."

"What's your point?" I asked.

"That's my point. Nobody's perfect. Not even Mom. She means well, but sometimes she's wrong."

His eyes concentrated on mine, and I suddenly felt uncomfortable.

I looked away and tried to steer the conversation back to where it began. "Are you going to see him again?"

"Yeah, we planned to keep in touch. His son doesn't know anything about me, so he needs to tell him. Next time I'm going to meet his son and his wife. My brother's name is Brian."

"What's Mom gonna think about that?"

"Right now, I don't care. It went well. I like him. I want to get to know his family— *my* family. I have a whole *family* that I've never met. I feel like Mom robbed me of that, you know? Like ... even if Jake wasn't a great dad, I could've still had grandparents, aunts, uncles and cousins who loved me."

"Wow," was all I could mutter. I felt bad. I'd always just considered Kevin to be my brother, and I never realized what it was like for him. My family on Doug's side wasn't his family, even though they were, in a sense. But all that time, he had other relatives somewhere, and he never had a chance to know them.

"Jake has two sisters and a brother, and they each have at least two kids. His parents own a big house at the beach, and every year they take a vacation together. Not that it's all about vacations ... I just feel like I missed out on a lot."

I nodded. There was nothing I could say.

***

Later that night, Mom and Kevin had another fight about Jake. It happened after dinner while I was trying to watch my favorite old sitcom on television. They started talking in the kitchen but migrated to the living room as their discussion turned into an argument. As they stood in front of me, there was no way to escape and I had a front-row seat for all the fireworks.

"Of course he'd say that!" Mom yelled. "He wants to make a good impression on you and turn me into the bad guy!"

"He didn't say anything bad about you," Kevin told her. "He actually said that you were a good person, and he was sorry that things turned out the way they did between you. He said it looks like you did a good job raising me."

"Oh, flattery, then!" she laughed sarcastically.

"It's not that—" Kevin started.

Mom interrupted, "You know, we wouldn't be having this problem if it weren't for your meddling girlfriend."

"Ginny didn't force me to do anything. Leave her out of this!"

"Right. She didn't force you. She just made the suggestion, didn't she? And now look at us! Perhaps you should rethink your relationship with that one."

"Mom, leave her out of this! Ginny didn't do anything wrong, and Jake is not a bad guy."

"Sure. If he's such a great person, where has he been all these years?" Mom demanded.

"Well, for the past ten years, he's been in the city with his wife and son. He's a chef, and his wife is a representative for a company that sells pools."

Mom brushed away Kevin's words. "That's not what I meant. I mean, why hasn't he contacted you? Why didn't he try to see you, if he regretted everything so much?"

"He did," Kevin told her. "About fifteen years ago, he called your parents and tried to get in touch with us. But they told him to take a hike, and they threatened legal action if he didn't comply. So he left us alone."

Mom stared and said nothing at first. Then she simply stated, "I wasn't aware of that."

"So you see?" Kevin asked. "He's not a monster."

Mom looked blank for a second and then her face took on a new emotion. "So, he makes one phone call and that makes it OK? If he cared so much, why didn't he keep trying? He could've hired a private investigator to find you, if he really cared!"

Kevin looked Mom in the eye and lowered his voice to a normal volume. "I know he wasn't perfect. He admitted to me that he screwed up. But he's not the only one. You messed up too, Mom. You made me grow up without half of my family. You taught me to hate people I didn't even know."

"I got you a new family!" Mom yelled as tears streamed down her face. "I gave you a *better* family. A new dad, a sister, a brother ... . I tried to fix it and give you what you should've had all along. Jake wasn't worthy of you. We were better off without him."

Kevin shook his head. "Were we? Really? All that time that I felt like a fifth wheel ... you were all part of something. But I was different. I was a foreigner. My brother and sister had a dad, and I didn't."

"Oh, Honey!" Mom cried, throwing her arms around Kevin. "You were always a part of us, even more than if you'd been traveling back and forth to see Jake. You had stability, and that's what's important."

Kevin shook his head, but still hugged her back. "It's OK, Mom," he said calmly. "You made a mistake, and I forgive you. I just want to move forward with the truth. It's not a competition. I can love you and Doug and even Jake and his family too, if it comes to that."

I sat there, frozen on the couch. I'd never seen my mom like that. She wasn't angry anymore, she was ... something else. She looked smaller, and Kevin seemed more like the parent. I tried to absorb everything that had just happened. I wanted to understand why Mom had kept Kevin from his father. I thought about what it must've been like for Jake and Kevin all those years. I was happy that Kevin had made the connection to Jake. At the same time, I was worried about how Mom felt and what this would do to our family.

***

The day before Kevin left, he took me out for lunch. At my request, we went to another coffee place, similar to the one he and Ginny took me to. I ordered a grilled cheese sandwich, soup and a cup of gourmet tea.

"Are you ready for me to leave?" Kevin asked as we sat down.

I laughed. "Kinda," I told him. "You really caused a ruckus, you know."

He smiled. "Nah, that will all blow over eventually. You'll see."

"I hope so," I told him. "You know how Mom can be."

"I do," he said seriously. "And I wanted to talk to you about that."

My stomach flip-flopped. I didn't say anything. I just looked at him.

Kevin cleared his throat. "Um, I just ... wanted to tell you ... you know, you're still my sister."

"Yeah, of course," I said. I was a little confused about why he was telling me that.

"Well, this whole thing with Jake .... I didn't want you to feel like I was rejecting you. I'm not. And that's what Mom thought, so I wanted to make sure I told you how I feel."

"I heard you when you told Mom it wasn't a competition," I told him. "I didn't think you would think I would think you were choosing them over us."

We both chuckled at my last sentence.

"I just wanted to make sure you didn't get that impression," he said. "Because I had my own reasons for meeting Jake, and they had nothing at all to do with you or Danny or your dad."

"But they had to do with Mom?" I asked.

"Just a little ... only because she was the one who told me those things about him. You'll see, Gina. Someday you'll start to question things people tell you. You'll want to find your own answers and decide things for yourself. And you should do that."

He was looking at me intently.

"OK," I said, nodding.

"You know," he began. "My situation is a lot like yours."

"What do you mean?" I asked.

"This whole thing with Jake. It's a lot like you and Doug, except you're older than I was. You haven't seen Doug or his family, just like I never saw Jake and his family."

I shook my head. "No, it's different," I told him. "You never met Jake. You didn't really know how he was. But I've seen how Doug is with Danny, and I know what he's done to Mom. I made my decision based on facts."

Kevin took a moment to finish chewing his food. "But still, you can only see one side," he suggested. "You haven't visited Doug or even spoken to him in months. You haven't listened to his side at all. So how do you know you're right?"

I felt anxious again. "I know enough." My voice sounded shaky. "I've heard the phone calls, and I've seen the paperwork from the lawyer. I've listened to the things

116

Danny says, and I've heard things other people have said about him."

Kevin sighed. "It must be horrible for you to be so close to their divorce."

I shrugged. "It's no different than when they were married, I guess. I just know more now. I understand more too. For a long time, I thought it was Mom's fault they were fighting. Now I see her side ... just like you said. Now I understand."

"Don't you miss him?" he asked.

"Sometimes," I confessed. "But I know better."

"I used to think that too, about Jake," Kevin said. "What about Doug's family? Do you miss them?"

I looked down at my plate and picked at the crusts of my sandwich. "I don't know ... they're all tied to him. And those grandparents are stuck up."

"You think so?" he asked me. "Because, I never felt that way about them. They were always nice to me, and they didn't have to be. I wasn't their grandchild, but they treated me like I was."

"Well, apparently they didn't approve of Mom when Doug started seeing her."

"Oh," Kevin nodded. "I heard about that. But I think they got over it, don't you? I mean ... for the past fourteen years they've been pretty good to our family."

I shrugged again, still looking at my mutilated lunch.

Kevin took the conversation in a new direction. "I feel bad," he told me. "I feel like ... if I had been home, then you wouldn't be going through this. Like, I could've shielded you from all that ugliness."

"I'm not a baby," I said, looking up at him. "Even Mom says I shouldn't be treated like a child."

"Yeah, well you're also not the one getting divorced. So you shouldn't have to deal with all the details."

I sat back in my chair and sighed. Even talking about the divorce was exhausting.

"I'm going to see Doug today," Kevin said. "You wanna tag along? I know he'd like to see you, and we don't have to tell Mom."

My stomach flip-flopped again. I didn't know what to say. It seemed so simple and harmless. But if Mom found out, her feelings would be hurt. I didn't want to upset her anymore. She was going through a lot, and she already felt like Kevin was leaving her. I couldn't do the same thing he did. Besides, what would I say to Doug? It had been such a long time. The last time I was anywhere near him was at the science fair and that wasn't a good experience. When I thought about it, he seemed like a stranger, and I had no reason to talk to him.

"No," I told him, shaking my head for emphasis. "You can drop me off at home before you go there."

***

Things returned to normal after Kevin went back to school. Mom relaxed a little more, and we fell into our standard routines. We didn't talk much about Kevin, and we didn't mention Jake or Ginny at all. I could tell she was still pretty sensitive about the issues attached to those names.

One Saturday while Danny was with Doug, Mom had some news for me. "I have a date tonight," she announced during lunch.

I was surprised. "Oh?" was all I could say.

She nodded.

"With who?"

"His name is Ben. I met him through Aunt Tamara."

"Where are you going?" I asked.

"To dinner, and we might meet up with Aunt Tamara and some friends for drinks." She was happy. I could tell by her voice.

"OK, that's cool. Um, what time?" I wanted to know. I felt like the mom, asking when she was leaving and coming home from her date.

"I'll be leaving to meet him around six o'clock, and I'm sure I'll be home before midnight," she told me.

"And it's OK if I stay here?" I asked.

She nodded. "I don't mind as long as you behave yourself. Mr. and Mrs. Lukoski are on the other side of the wall if you need anything."

"What are you going to wear?" I wanted to know.

Mom smiled a little. "I'm not sure," she began. "I was hoping you could help me with that after lunch."

I smiled too. I was glad Mom was going to let me help her get ready for her special night.

I helped Mom select an outfit and jewelry. Then we did a mini-facial, and I painted her nails while she had mud on her face. It was a lot of fun, and we giggled a lot. I hadn't seen Mom so happy in a long time. It felt good to see her excited about something.

She asked that I not tell Danny about her date and said that even if things went well, we wouldn't meet Ben for a long time because she wanted to be sure they were serious. Mostly, she was worried about Danny getting confused. I told her she could trust me to keep her secret. After all, we were friends. When six o'clock came, she went out the door looking like a million bucks. I was proud of her.

I was watching a movie on the couch when she came home five hours later. She hurried in the door and sat down with me.

"So? How was it?" I asked.

Mom sighed. "I had such a good time!" she exclaimed. "Ben was the perfect gentleman. We had a fantastic dinner at a restaurant he picked. We sat and talked for hours. It was so ... nice!"

"Then you're going to see him again?"

"Yes. He's going to call me this week so we can set something up." Mom was glowing.

"Well, tell me about him!" I was happy for her. After everything she'd been through, she was finally smiling.

"Um, let's see .... He's my age. He's an accountant. He's been divorced for three years, and he has a daughter who is ten. He likes to go for walks, and he coaches his daughter's soccer team. He prefers red wine. He's been to Europe. He was raised on a farm. And he loves ice cream!" Mom giggled.

"That's great!" I said. "Did he kiss you goodnight?"

She blushed. "A lady never tells," she said as she stood up. "Now, I'm going upstairs to call Aunt Tamara. I'll see you in the morning, OK?"

I nodded. "I'm glad you had fun," I told her.

Mom smiled. "Me too. It's been a long time."

Chapter 9: February

Mom and Ben started communicating heavily as the weeks passed. It seemed she always had her phone in her hand, either sending or receiving a message of some sort. At night, after Danny went to bed, they would call each other, and she would disappear into her room. She seemed happier than I ever remembered seeing her. Danny noticed too, but he didn't know the reason behind her non-stop smiling.

One Friday night, after Danny went with Doug, Mom called Aunt Tamara to chat while she was getting ready for her date with Ben. I could hear her from my room as she paced the hallway between her bedroom and the bathroom.

"Yes, I think so. I'm a little nervous."

"Well, his place, obviously."

"I know. I do. It would be nice."

"I see what you mean."

"Yeah, he knows. He seemed pretty upset about it."

"Well, he ... you know. So I think it really hit home for him. He said he would be devastated if it happened to him."

"Yeah, I told him. But we didn't talk about it too long. He was noticeably upset about it, like he thought I had something to do with it or I have power over the situation between the two of them. It wasn't pleasant."

"No, most people are supportive. I was surprised."

"I have. And you know the whole situation with Kevin plays into this too. He brought that up as well. I don't know ... I used to be so sure and now I just ... I don't know."

"I got more letters from the lawyers today. He's still pushing me about the visitation issue. He wants to finalize the division of assets and get the divorce over with, but he doesn't want to let that one go."

"No, that's what my lawyer recommended."

"I know. That's another thing. I'm really feeling good now, and I'm ready to put it all behind me. I don't exactly want to go through all that nor do I want to put the kids through it."

"Oh, I don't think it's that simple. Right now, though, I wish it were."

"Talk to Doug? You know I don't want to do that."

"Yes, it's cheaper, but that doesn't make it easier."

"Mmm hmm."

"Yeah."

"I know. You're right. It's just ... ugh, this downward spiral. I'm so far into it now I can't even think about how to turn it around. I haven't had a conversation with him in months. We've just ... just retrained ourselves, I guess."

"Right, to the tune of several thousand dollars!"

"His was easy. He said they talked a lot through the process, and it went smoothly. He only spent a fraction of what I've shelled out so far."

"Yeah, well with just one child, it was easier to keep their focus on her, I think."

"Yes, they do. It's weird. She actually stopped by his house one night while we were on the phone."

"It was fine. He didn't care. She was picking up or dropping off some item for Cassie. They were friendly to each other."

"I don't know. It's very strange to me. Normal people don't do that, do they? I mean, she was in his house. They talk on the phone too."

"No, actually she's engaged."

"Yeah, that's fine too. Ben met him a long time ago and after the engagement happened, they all went out to dinner together."

"He said he wants her to believe that her family is growing through the process instead of shrinking. He doesn't like phrases like *broken home* and *single parent*. He says they give people the wrong idea. His child has three parental figures right now, and he thinks that's great for her."

"It's just so different from me. It's completely the opposite of how I feel."

"Well, I've never met his daughter, but from what he tells me she's happy and well-adjusted, so I guess it's healthy for her. At least right now."

"Right. Utopian."

"I know, I need to get going too."

"Of course I will. Thanks."

"Yup, buh-bye."

I couldn't understand everything they'd been talking about. However, the part about Ben's relationship with his ex-wife was obvious. Ben believed his daughter's family would grow as a result of his divorce, and Mom had said that was the opposite of how she felt. It was certainly the opposite of how I saw things too. Since the divorce, my family got smaller.

I wondered what it would be like if my parents were as friendly as Ben and his ex-wife. I thought about his daughter, Cassie, and what her life was like. She didn't have to choose between her parents or worry how each of them felt. She could retrieve belongings from her dad even when she wasn't staying with him. And her family celebrated big changes together. I thought that must be nice for her. For a moment, I was jealous. Then I thought about my friends and how bored I'd become with them because they seemed so much younger than me. I imagined Cassie was probably like that too. She most likely didn't understand lawyers and courts and paperwork and assets. I was still better off in my situation.

Mom stopped in my room before she left. "I might be later than usual tonight," she told me. "Don't wait up, OK?"

"OK," I said. "Have fun with Ben."

Mom flashed me a big smile and then disappeared down the hall. "There are leftovers in the fridge!" she called before she went out the door.

I stood up and stretched. I looked in the mirror and thought about what to do for the evening. I could deep-condition my hair and put a mud mask on my face. Or I could watch a movie ... or two. I could call Sarah or Jenny and see if they were up to anything. I thought about Danny and wondered how he was going to be spending the evening. I thought about Kevin and wondered how things were going for him. That was when I decided to call Kevin just to chat.

"Gina?" he said when he answered the phone. "What's up?"

"Oh, nothing," I told him. "Mom's on a date, and I was bored."

"A date?" he sounded surprised. "Really?"

"You hadn't heard? She's been seeing an accountant named Ben since last month. She's really happy with him."

"Wow. That's ... um, great, I guess." Kevin was a little shocked by the news. "How do you feel about him?"

"I haven't met him, so I don't know."

"Does he have any kids?" Kevin wanted to know.

I filled him in on the situation with Ben's ex-wife and daughter and his ex's fiancé. Then I told him not to tell anyone because I'd only heard Mom say all those things to Aunt Tamara over the phone. I didn't want Mom to find out what a snoop I was.

"That sounds fantastic!" Kevin exclaimed when I was finished.

"Fantastic?" I didn't understand why he thought so. "It's kinda weird, don't you think?"

"No, I don't. I think it's great. I mean, think about his daughter. She hasn't had to go through any of the crap you did. Or me, for that matter, in my situation."

"How is Jake?" I asked.

"Good," Kevin said. "I connected with Brian and Elaina online, and we've been trading pictures and stories. It's going well."

"That's awesome," I told him.

"I know. It's awesome now, but it shouldn't have been this way. If Mom hadn't pulled away when I was little ... if she would've let me see Jake, we wouldn't have this gap to fill. It sounds like her new boyfriend might be a good influence on her."

"Are you mad?"

I heard Kevin take a deep breath. "No. I'm ... ah, *irritated*, or something. Every day now I think about how Mom could've done things differently and made everything better. But then I think that she didn't know any better and she was doing what she thought was the right thing, so I can't be mad. I just want everything to be OK. And I don't want you to go through what I went through."

"Don't worry about me," I said. "I'm fine. I can take care of myself."

"OK," Kevin sighed. "What else is new? How's school going?"

We talked for about a half hour. He said that Ginny asked about me, and he would tell her I said hi. He also said that his roommate had decided to transfer to a different school in the fall. I loved hearing about Kevin's life at college. I felt dumb telling him the same old stuff that was going on in my life.

After I got off the phone, I plodded to the kitchen, found some cold mashed potatoes in the fridge, and made my way to the couch for the evening.

***

I slept late the next morning and woke up around ten o'clock. I heard Mom downstairs and decided to go say hello and see how her date was.

"Good morning," I yawned as I entered the kitchen.

Mom was sitting at the table with her laptop. "Hi, Honey," she said without looking up.

"So?" I asked, sitting down with a bowl of cereal. "How was your night with Ben?"

Mom pursed her lips and shook her head a little. "Not so great, actually." She looked up. "Gina, I think we need to talk about something."

I got that hollow feeling in my stomach and my throat. I put down my spoon. "Yeah?" I asked.

"You need to start seeing your father," she said. "This has gone on long enough."

I was confused. I thought she liked the fact that she and I were a team. I didn't say anything at first. I just stared, searching her eyes for some clarification. Her gaze was firm on me, and she didn't say anything else.

"What?" I finally choked out.

"I think you need to start seeing your dad. What you're doing to him isn't fair. In fact, it's caused a lot of problems, and it's time to stop."

"What?" I asked again. "You said you supported me."

Mom sighed, "You're right. I did say that." She seemed to soften a little. "But I was wrong, Gina. I shouldn't have allowed you to refuse to see him."

I was stunned. "I don't get it. You said it was OK! You told me it was my decision. You even told other people that you were proud of me! And your friends were proud of me!"

"Oh, Honey. I'm sorry. I know this must be confusing for you."

"Yeah. Yeah, it's confusing. You said he was bad. You said he wasn't a good father, and now you're telling me to go see him? After you said I was more mature than he is ... Why?"

"I know ..." Mom shook her head and wiped the corner of her eye with her fingertips. "Honey, I was very angry when your father left. I felt like he abandoned us, and I didn't want to be alone and—"

"Oh my gosh. Is this about Ben?" Things were beginning to click in my mind. "You want me to go away so you can be alone with Ben, don't you? Now that you have him, you don't need me around to keep you company!"

"I would be lying if I said that Ben had nothing to do with this, but—"

"But *nothing*!" I was seething. "I can't believe you would do this to me. I thought we were friends, and now I'm not good enough for you since you have a boyfriend?"

"Gina, you are my daughter, and you're twelve years old. We aren't schoolgirls, and I'm not getting rid of you because I have a boyfriend. I'm trying to explain that—"

"No!" I shouted as I stood up. "You don't have to explain anything. I get it. I'm not stupid. I can see people for who they are! You even said so yourself. Or was that a lie too?"

Mom began to raise her voice. "Gina, I am your mother. Listen to me—"

"NO! I am *sick* of listening to you. I've been listening to you for months, and I've been worrying about you and wondering if you're OK. I've been here for you when nobody else was because you needed me. I took care of Danny to keep him out of your way because you were having a hard time. I don't care *who* you say you are now. You're not who I thought you were!" I pushed my chair in with too much force, and the table shook. Some of my cereal spilled over the edge of the bowl, but I didn't care. I glared at Mom for a moment and then ran upstairs to my room.

I slammed the door and fell on my bed, sobbing. I didn't know what to do, and I didn't know who to trust. I didn't understand why Mom had changed her mind about Doug. I couldn't believe she wanted to get rid of me so she could spend time with Ben.

Mom came up the stairs after me. She knocked on my door and then walked into my room.

"Get OUT!" I screamed, throwing a pillow at her.

She stood straight and calmly said, "No."

"I don't want to see you," I continued, my voice still raised in anger. "I don't want to talk to you. I don't want to hear any more about your boyfriend or your divorce or my father. I want to be left alone!"

"Well, that's too bad, Gina." Mom was still standing in the middle of my room. "I'm not going to leave this room until we've said everything we need to say."

"Then I'll leave!" I shouted. "I'll jump out the window like you told Doug I'd do at his apartment!"

"I don't think that's wise. Do you?" She took a step closer to my bed.

My nose was running, and my hair was in my eyes. I wiped my face with my sleeve. "What do you want?"

"We need to have a very serious discussion. I'd prefer you remain calm, however, I understand if you are unable to control yourself."

Unable to control myself? Did she think I was a toddler?

"Fine," I said.

"Honey, I'm sorry."

"For what?" I asked. My words were sharp.

"For everything. I'm sorry that things didn't work out in my marriage to your dad. I'm sorry we had to move out of our house. I'm sorry you had to do so much babysitting. I'm sorry ... " She took a deep breath. "I'm sorry that I put you in a position where you felt you had to choose a side and act like an adult. That was wrong of me. As a parent, I made a huge mistake."

I was still confused. "But you never *told* me to choose sides! And you said from the beginning that I was mature. *I* made the decision not to see Doug! You even said so yourself. You didn't force me to do anything. You were honest with me and let me make up my mind. And I did. And you were OK with it until now."

Mom shook her head. "I know, I ... oh ... Honey, I love you so much. When your dad left, I was afraid you'd want to go with him. You two were always so close. And I was scared and lonely, and suddenly I was a single mom, and the only thing I wanted more than anything was to hold my family together."

"Then why didn't you try to work things out?" I wanted to know. I didn't think she was making sense.

"It's not that simple," she began again. "Your dad and I had been trying to work things out for years. When he said we needed a divorce, I knew he was right. He wanted to do what was best for you and Danny because we were fighting all the time. And he was right! I didn't want to put you through that either."

"Then why did you keep fighting after he left?"

"Oh, lots of reasons. Honestly? I kinda missed him. And at the same time, I was angry, and I blamed him for how difficult things had become. I wanted to hurt him because it seemed like he had it so easy ... and ... well, I guess I did."

"What do you mean?" I asked.

"I mean he got hurt. And it felt good to me. When you stopped seeing him, it was like I won and he was paying for what he did. I took that as a sign that I was right, and then I kept going because I had confidence in what I was doing. Do you understand?"

I shook my head.

"I should never, ever, have let you hear those negative things about your dad. I shouldn't have let you have a choice about seeing him. He's your father, and he loves you. I had no right to come between you."

"So you're saying you should have forced me to spend time with some lazy jerk who didn't care about me?"

"No, Gina. Your father isn't a lazy jerk. He does care about you, and he would never intentionally let anything bad happen to you."

"But you said—"

"I know what I said. And I'm telling you I was wrong. You know that sometimes people say things they don't mean because they're upset. I shouldn't have said those things about your dad ... or his family. They are *your* family, and you have every right to see them and love them and enjoy yourself with them. Remember all those things Kevin said about how much he missed out on by not seeing Jake?"

I nodded.

"I don't want you to feel the same way in a couple years. And if this continues, you will feel that way. Because, Gina, I've been treating you like an adult, but you're not an adult. Some day you will look back on this and realize that what you really needed was a mother to help you through this process. That's where I've failed you. And I want that to end right now."

After months of stating otherwise, Mom was saying she wanted to start treating me like a child.

"I'm not a little kid," I told her.

"I know. You're almost a teenager. And I realize there's a delicate balance between the freedom you deserve and the structure you need."

I wrinkled my face at her, and she shook her head. "Never mind. I'm saying that you and I are probably going to have some rough times ahead of us. And that's why I think it's important that we talk about these things to make sure we understand each other."

"I still don't understand," I said. "You said that you were wrong and I have to start seeing Doug. But what about how I feel? Don't you care about that anymore? Now you're going to boss me around?"

"I realize this has been a lot for you. And it was a rather unexpected way to spend your morning. How do you feel right now?"

Even though part of me missed my dad, I wasn't ready to see him. "I feel like I don't even know Doug anymore.

How am I supposed to go stay at his apartment— the *trashcan*— again?"

Mom winced. "For starters, you can stop calling him 'Doug' and refer to him as your 'dad' again," she said. "And I know there's a big gap, so I imagine we'll have to take it slow." She paused to take a breath. "I think I might consult a professional to help us."

I really didn't feel too great after hearing that. "You mean some stranger is going to tell me what to do?"

"Shhh," Mom lowered her voice so I would calm down. "It's not like that. And I'm not sure if that's what we'll do or not. I'll need to talk to your dad, and we can decide together what's best ... for *all* of us."

"Wait," I couldn't believe what I was hearing. "You're going talk to Dou ... Dad ... and decide together? Don't you hate him?"

"Well, I don't want to be married to your father anymore, that's true. But the one thing we have in common is that we both love you and want what's best for you. So I think I can handle working through this with him."

"I just don't get it," I muttered. "I still think you're trying to get rid of me because of Ben."

Mom nodded. "I know it must look that way, doesn't it? But that's not the case. Actually, it was Ben who said you should see your father, not me. His family situation is much different than ours, and he was quite disturbed when I told him that you don't have regular visits with your dad."

"So, you're doing this because you don't want to lose him?" There was too much going on in my head. I couldn't make sense of any of it, and the longer we talked, the more confused I became.

"Not at all, Honey. Ben and I had a very long talk last night, and he made me see things from his perspective ... which, allowed me to have some more compassion for your dad. I realized I was wrong about a lot, and I did things that hurt people I love."

"What do you mean? I'm not hurt."

"Not that you can tell. But Gina, you are half me and half your dad. We made you. You know how that works. So, if you hate your dad ... well, that means you hate part of yourself. I don't know if you realize it or not, but that's what it translates to."

"So, Ben just changed your mind about everything? In a couple hours he changed ... like, *everything* you've been saying for months?"

"It sounds weird, doesn't it? I think this has been stewing inside me since December when Kevin called Jake. But it really came together last night. And ... I ... well, I know I messed up. And I know there's work to do. I don't know about these things because I've never been in this situation. So ... can you bear with me? Can you forgive me for all the confusion?"

I felt drained. I didn't know what to say.

"You know, how about if we take a break for a while?" Mom asked. She began to move toward the door again. "I'll give you some time to think and talk to your friends or whatever you need to do. Why don't you let me know when you're ready to talk again? I'm sure you'll think of more questions."

I nodded. "OK," I said. I was relieved to have a break. It was too heavy to deal with all at once.

After Mom closed the door and I heard her go downstairs, I stood up and went to my closet. I reached far into the left side and dug into the cardboard box I'd stuffed back there. A moment later, I pulled out Henry-The-Stuffed-Bunny. I took him to my bed and laid down. While clutching Henry to my chest, I closed my eyes and fell asleep.

***

The following Thursday evening, I stayed home with Danny while Mom met my dad for coffee. She had asked him if they could talk about the current situation and what they could do to improve it. From what I understood, Ben was going to join them as well.

I felt irritable all evening. I didn't like the idea of my parents sitting around with my mom's boyfriend and talking about me while I wasn't there. I'd never even met Ben! I also didn't like the way Mom had been treating me. She'd even made a new rule that I needed to go to bed before ten o'clock on school nights.

I made sure Danny took a bath and was properly dressed in his pajamas. I double-checked his homework and quizzed him on his spelling words. Then I gave him a snack and put him to bed at eight-thirty.

"Gina?" Danny asked as I was turning out the light.

"Yeah?" I turned the light back on.

"Do you think Mommy and Daddy are going to fight at the resternot?"

"You mean, the *restaurant*?" I corrected him.

Danny nodded.

I shook my head. "No. I don't think they'll fight in public. Actually, I think that's why they chose to meet in a public place."

Danny sighed. "OK."

"Are you worried?" I asked him.

"No. I just didn't want them to get arrested."

"Arrested?" I was surprised. "What made you think of that?"

He yawned. "I saw it on TV once. People were fighting, and they threw food, and the police came."

I laughed as I imagined my parents covered in spaghetti and soup. "I don't think that's going to happen," I said. "Now get some sleep, OK? I'll see you in the morning."

Danny smiled, rolled over on his side, and closed his eyes. I shut off the light and closed the door.

In the hallway, I giggled again at the thought of Mom and Dad having a food fight. Then I wondered how their conversation was going, and I started to feel a little nervous. It had been a long time since I'd seen them share a room without fighting.

Mom came home at nine-thirty. I was watching old sitcoms when she walked in.

"How did it go?" I asked.

"Well, it was a little awkward at first. But then it got better. It helped having Ben there. He and your father got along very well."

"Why?" I wanted to know.

"Well, they're both divorced dads ... Well, *almost* divorced, in your dad's case. I guess that's the biggest thing. And Ben was there to tell your father his views on divorce and parenthood. I think your dad appreciated it a lot."

"So what did you say about me?" There was an edgy tone in my voice, but I couldn't help it.

"Gina, it wasn't all about you," Mom began. "The real issues are between me and your father."

"OK, so did Ben help you and Dad have a better relationship?" For some reason, I felt like crying. I could tell things were going to be different again, and I was scared about what might come next.

"No. Ben didn't stay long. We all had a nice chat. He spoke about his experience, and then he left me and Dad to hash things out."

"Did you?"

"We did a pretty good job. We talked about a lot of things, beginning with apologies. I think we made some progress."

"What kind of progress? What's going to happen now?" I demanded to know.

"Well, for starters, Dad and I are going to begin seeing a divorce coach to help us work together and be better co-parents. We'll be sharing more information with each other, so you can expect Dad to be a more prominent figure in your life from now on."

I felt like someone dropped a brick in my stomach. "But Mom! I haven't talked to him in months!"

"I know." She reached out and touched my forearm. "We talked about that too. Your dad is going to start interviewing therapists, and then we'll set up some time for you and him to begin rebuilding your relationship."

"A therapist? You said there was nothing wrong with me! You told him that! And now you want me to go to a therapist with him? Why???" I couldn't believe what I was hearing. After everything that had happened, everything Mom had said ... she had completely changed her mind about all of it. How did she expect me to react?

"Calm down," Mom said. "Dad and I agreed that a therapist's office would be a healthy place for the two of you to talk again. A professional will be there to help you communicate and identify any issues you might need to work through."

I started to cry. Everything was changing, and I didn't like it. I was scared to see my dad again. I was even more afraid of going to therapy. "Was this Ben's idea? It's his fault, isn't it?!?" I shouted through my tears.

"Ben made some recommendations based on his experience. But he wasn't there when your father and I made these decisions." "Why aren't you going to therapy with Dad?" I wanted to know. "You're the one who said

136

you screwed up. It was your problems that caused all of this. You said so!"

"Not that it's any of your concern, but I will likely begin seeing a therapist by myself," she told me. "Your father and I decided to see a coach together because we need to work on an action plan. We need to move forward. Our relationship as it was is over, and it's time to focus on the business at hand."

I grabbed a tissue from the end table and wiped my eyes. "When do I need to go to the therapist?"

"We'll wait until your dad finds someone he's comfortable with. It's important to check around and make sure we choose someone qualified to help you in your situation."

I sat still for a moment and then another flood of tears came. I broke down sobbing and buried my face in my hands. Mom put her arms around me.

"Oh, Honey," her voice started to crack. "I'm sorry. I'm so, so sorry."

Chapter 10: March

My dad chose a female therapist named Dee. Our first appointment was on a Wednesday night. Mom got a sitter for Danny, and she drove me to Dee's office after work. She told me she would only do that in the beginning and soon I'd have to ride with my dad.

Dee had a big smile and a terrific sense of fashion. She shook my hand as I walked in the door, and I immediately felt welcome. Her office was painted light blue, and there were a lot of pictures of the ocean on the walls. I sat in a comfy leather chair while my dad took a seat on the couch. Dee rolled her chair out from behind her desk so she was sitting directly in front of us. I liked her better that way. She seemed less intimidating. Still, I felt out of place. After we got settled, I began picking at my nail polish.

Dee spoke first. She spent several minutes telling us about herself. She talked about where she went to school. She told us about her professional background and why she made the choice to work with "evolving" families.

"Now, Gina," she began. "I know a little about you from what your dad has told me, but I'd really like to hear from you. What can you tell me about yourself?"

I told Dee how old I was and where I went to school. I said that I was a night-owl, I got good grades, and I liked to read. She asked about bunnies and the color yellow. I confirmed that I still liked both of those things.

I thought I'd have to talk about why I hadn't wanted to see my dad, but Dee didn't bring up the past. She did tell me that if I wanted to, I could schedule some private sessions for just the two of us, and we could discuss anything that was bothering me. For the rest of our time there, we talked about things that my dad and I had in common, books and movies we liked, and games we played. We also talked about what was going on with his family. I was excited to hear that my new cousin was due to be born the following month.

The time went fast and before I knew it, our session was over. Dee smiled at me again, told me it was a pleasure to meet me, and said she looked forward to seeing us the following week. I felt relieved that I'd gotten through it. I was also surprised at how comfortable I was. I was even a little disappointed to leave. After I'd gotten used to it, the office felt like a safe escape from my normal life.

We returned to the waiting area where Mom was sitting next to a big saltwater fish tank. She looked up and smiled at both of us as we walked through the door.

"Hi," she said. "That went fast. Did you like Dee?"

I nodded. "It wasn't so bad," I told her.

She turned to my dad. "So, next week, we should meet you again? Same time, same place?"

"Yes." My dad smiled. "Thanks again, Jill. I feel good about this."

Mom reached out and shook Dad's hand. "We'll see you next week."

It was odd to see my parents shake hands. The three of us blushed and shared an awkward giggle.

On the way home, Mom asked if I wanted to talk about the session.

"There's not much to say," I told her. "We talked about movies and the time we built a castle out of wooden blocks."

"Were you comfortable?" she asked. "I know you were worried about seeing a therapist."

"It was OK. I don't know what I expected. But ... like, she wasn't dressed like a doctor. And her office was really pretty."

"Well, I'm glad." Mom glanced over at me. "I think this is the beginning of something good."

I wondered what she meant by that. Again, I wondered if she wanted me to see my dad because it meant she could spend more time with Ben. I was beginning to feel like I was less important to her.

"What about Ben?" I asked.

Mom wrinkled her forehead. "What do you mean?"

"Well, I know this was all his idea ... so ... am I ever going to meet him or something?"

"Hmmm ... Ben and I discussed that," she told me. "But I think it's still a little too soon. You're going through a big change right now. Ben and I have a very new relationship, and I don't want Danny to get confused."

"So why does Dad get to meet him, but I don't? I'm closer to you than he is."

"Your father met him as part of an adult discussion. You're our daughter. It's different."

"Why is it different? You used to say that I shouldn't be treated like a child. So why are you treating me like one now?"

Mom sighed. "Gina, this is a sensitive issue. Don't forget Ben has a daughter too. We're trying to be considerate of all of our children."

"There you go again!" I raised my voice. "You called me a child. Why are you treating me this way now that Ben is in the picture?"

"You are a child," she said sternly. "I know I previously made comments and said you shouldn't be treated the same as your brother, and that's true. But you're still not an adult. I *am* an adult, and I will make these decisions. I love you and your brother. I want what's best for you. I don't want to put you in a situation that is unsteady and may cause further ... issues," she finished.

I sat back in my seat and folded my arms. I didn't like these new changes. I didn't like being treated like a little kid. I didn't like not knowing what was going on. I felt like she cut me out of a big part of her life and, after everything I'd done for her, I didn't understand why.

***

Later that night, I went to bed when I was told to. I was just beginning to drift off to sleep when I heard Mom on the phone downstairs. I opened my eyes and crept to the door.

" ... seemed to go well. At least while they were there," she was saying.

"Oh, it was weird. But a good weird. I shook his hand afterward. He was very appreciative of my cooperation, and he said he thinks this will be a good thing."

"Yeah. I don't know ... I think he might be the least of my problems right now. Gina seems to be testing me. She started another fight with me on the way home. She wants to meet Ben ... I think. I'm not quite sure what she really wants. I don't know if she does either."

"I realize that. I know it's hard for her. And I have given her somewhat of a demotion around here. She has a bedtime again. I've stopped discussing many of my issues with her. I think she's still adjusting."

"Oh, I know. I screwed up by giving her so much freedom. I just ... oh, I don't know ... I thought she deserved it, I guess. And I certainly wasn't in a position to be strong and stern. It was just easier to let her take more liberties and step up the way she did. I thought I was lucky that I had such a mature kid."

"I know. Do you remember when you got Rocket, and we were reading that dog training manual?"

"Do you remember that it said the dog needs to understand who the boss is before it can relax and let you take the lead?"

"Well, kind of. I think it's the same principle, don't you? I mean, she seems concerned about things that aren't any of her business. She needs to learn that I can handle those issues ... that I'm the parent. I think she'll feel better when she can believe that I'm in control."

"I have no idea. She hasn't expressed any interest in seeing the therapist by herself. If it would help, I'm all for it. I don't want to get caught in this web of therapy, though. You know what I mean?"

"Yeah, that's what I like about the coaching that Doug and I are doing. It's very task-oriented. We talk about what we need to do and what the best way is to do it. That's it. No tangling of the past like when we went to marriage counseling."

"Right. We haven't talked about his mother at all."

"He's fine. He's happy about all of this. More happy than me, I think. But, you know he's got a different perspective. And he's had more time to think about these things."

"He's worried about the same things I am. He hasn't had a serious girlfriend since he and his ex split, so he hasn't introduced Cassie to anyone. He's worried about how she'll react when she realizes that she'll have to share him. Apparently, it's more difficult for children when their father finds a new partner, so he expects this to be much harder than her mother's engagement."

"I don't know exactly. It has something to do with men being providers and children don't want to share the provisions with anyone else."

"I told him that too. He reads a lot about the subject because he wants to understand the dynamics of his family."

"I know. I do too. Anyway, enough about me. How was your spa retreat?"

"Oh, I had one of those facials a few years ago. Do they still ..."

I turned from the door and tiptoed back to my bed. I didn't like what I heard. I couldn't believe my mom was comparing me to my aunt's dog! And she actually used the word "demoted." I felt sick and empty. I tried to cry, but no tears came. I wanted to scream, but that would've gotten me in trouble. I pulled the covers up, closed my eyes, and counted 462 sheep before I finally fell asleep.

***

A week later Mom drove me back to Dee's office for my second session with Dad. When we got into the office, I sat in the chair again, and Dad sat on the couch. Dee asked us some questions about how we were feeling and if anything was new since the last time we saw her. Then she asked if either of us had anything we wanted to talk about.

When I didn't say anything, Dad put up his hand as if he were in school and said that he wanted to know why I began refusing to see him.

Dee turned to me. "That's a good question," she said. "Can you tell your dad what made you change your mind about visiting him?"

I stared at my hands. A million thoughts were whirling in my head, and I couldn't pick any one reason.

Dee must've sensed that because she changed the question a little. "Many kids whose parents get divorced are angry because they don't have answers to something they want to know. Is there anything you'd like to ask your dad right now?"

"Umm ..." I thought out loud. "Who is your girlfriend?" I finally asked. "And why do you keep her a secret?"

Dad sighed and shook his head. "I don't have a girlfriend," he told me. "But if I did, I might not tell you about her until I was sure how I felt. I'd have to make sure any woman I date is worthy of meeting my kids."

"Mom told me you were seeing someone!" I felt my face get hot. "She said that you had a girlfriend, and she had red hair and drove a convertible and that she was a lot younger than you!"

Dad sighed again. "Gina, is that what started this?"

I looked down. "I don't know," I mumbled.

Dad continued. "I do remember that evening last fall when your mom called to ask me about the redhead in the convertible. She wasn't my girlfriend. She was just a friend, a co-worker, actually. I had some trouble with my car that day, and I had to have it towed to the garage. She was driving by and saw me on the side of the road, so she stopped. Then she gave me a ride home. It was nothing. She was just being nice."

"Mom said that you were being secretive. She tried to find out what was going on so she could tell me, and you wouldn't tell her!"

"That's right. I didn't tell your mother because it wasn't any of her concern. And I told her that. I also told her that it wasn't anything that concerned you or your brother."

"But if you didn't have anything to hide, why didn't you just tell her the truth?"

"Because, your mom and I aren't together anymore. We're supposed to be moving on, not checking up on each other. I didn't want your mom to think that she could call me and demand to know what's going on in my life. And if I had responded to her questions that night, I would have been inviting her to interrogate me again."

"So you just let everyone think you were seeing someone? You didn't bother telling me the truth?"

"I'm sorry." Dad's voice grew quiet. "I had no clue that things would turn out this way. I thought I would see you and we'd have some time together to straighten things out. We always talked before, so I wasn't worried. But then it was like a big snowball effect. Every time I wanted to see you, you rejected me or your mom got between us and wouldn't let me speak to you. Eventually, I didn't know why you were angry or what I could say to make things better. It seemed like everything I did was wrong."

Tears came to my eyes. "But you didn't even *try*!" I accused him. "You knew my phone number. You could've sent me a letter in the mail. You could've told Danny to tell me ... but you didn't. You just kept seeing Danny like I didn't exist, and every once in a while I'd hear from you."

Dad started to cry too. "Honey, I didn't know what to say or do. At the time, I didn't know exactly what the problem was because there was so much going on. I was confused, and I didn't want to make things worse. I wanted to give you the time and space you needed to see things clearly. But it seemed like there was never enough time. And every time I did try to reach out to you, you were so mean ... it hurt me. I'm sorry, Gina. Part of me was afraid of you."

I didn't know what to say. Dad was breaking down, and I felt terrible for making him so upset. I was also confused about what he'd said. He was the parent, and I was his kid. It didn't make any sense that he would be afraid of me. As we sat there sniffling, Dee handed each of us a box of tissues.

"Gina?" Dee asked me. "How do you feel about that?"

I wiped my eyes again and looked at her. "I don't know," I said. "I ... I'm ..." With that, I was overcome by another fit of tears.

Dad moved to the end of the couch that was closest to me and stretched out his hand. I took it and followed when he tugged on my arm. He pulled me into his lap and wrapped his arms around me. I felt like something inside me cracked open. I laid my head on his shoulder as every emotion spilled from me in the form of violent sobs. Dad held me tighter and rocked me the way he did when I was a little girl. I don't know how long we sat there and cried together.

When the sobbing subsided, Dee spoke. "I think that's enough work for today," she told us.

I'd forgotten that she was there. When I remembered where I was, I felt a little silly. I looked at Dee, and she smiled encouragingly at me.

"Would you like to use the restroom?" she asked.

I nodded, and she led me out the door and down the hall to a pretty bathroom with lush towels and expensive hand soap. I locked the door behind me and looked in the mirror. My face was red, my eyes were puffy, and my hair was matted on the right side. I was a mess. I splashed some water on my face and fixed my hair. Within a few minutes, I felt ready to walk back into the world.

I met Dad and Dee in the hallway. It was time to leave.

"Feel better?" Dee asked.

"Yes," I told her. "Thank you."

"You're welcome. I'll see you two next week, OK?"

I nodded. Dad thanked Dee and put his arm around me as we walked the rest of the way down the hall and through the door to the waiting room.

***

The next few days were confusing. I spent a lot of time feeling angry about everything. I was mad at my mom for trying to butt into Dad's business and causing our problems. Again, I felt angry at my dad for not trying harder to contact me and tell me the truth. I wanted to know more about other issues, like my dad's family and how well he cared for Danny. I was mad at Danny for being happy and oblivious. And, I was mad at Ben for changing Mom's mind. If I'd gone on hating my dad, things would've been the same. And easier.

I had a hard time concentrating at school. My friends wanted to know what was wrong, but they asked too many questions when I tried to talk to them. I found it was easier to keep my distance from people.

Over the weekend I heard Mom on the phone with Aunt Tamara. She was talking about my dad, so I listened.

"The coaching is still going fine."

"Yeah, he seems pretty happy about it."

"Two, so far. I'm not sure."

"Well, I don't know. She just seems ... off. Quiet. She's been spending a lot of time in her room. She's not chatting about her friends."

"I know. Maybe they're growing apart."

"I hope it's good for her. I mean, I don't want to send her to some, quote, *professional* who is going to make things worse. Right now, I don't like what I'm seeing. And remember last week? She was difficult on the way home."

"I know, it's a lot."

"No, I haven't."

"She doesn't say much. She doesn't have to tell me anything and neither does he. And that's awkward, you know? It's like they're in a secret club and I'm an outsider."

"But at least then I was in their presence .... I don't know. I guess it's just something I have to get used to. I'll put that on the list of things to work through with my therapist."

"No, I don't think I'm ready to pull her out. She hasn't said she doesn't like it. Doug said that he was warned about the amount of time it can take."

"No, I haven't told her how I feel. I've wanted to, but ... you know, that's counterproductive, I guess. She doesn't owe me anything based on my feelings. I think that's how we got into this mess."

"He thinks it's great. He said the same thing: they have a lot to work through, and it might be a little like a roller coaster for a while."

"Right, I know. He said it's not about me."

"I don't know what my role is supposed to be. Things are better with Doug, but I still don't love him. I don't know exactly what I'm supposed to do to support and encourage them given the fact that I don't want to have the kind of relationship with him that she needs to."

"I could do that, but that's even more therapy. And more bills!"

"No, that's stopped. Completely. The negotiations are done, and we're just waiting for the final paperwork."

"Yeah, it's amazing how quickly everything gets wrapped up when you run out of money."

"I know. And I spent entirely too much time telling him things that had nothing to do with the legalities of our separation."

"Ha, I think I heard that in a country song."

I wondered if Mom knew that I listened to her phone conversations. She had to know I could hear her because she was always complaining about how thin the walls were. I knew she felt left out when it came to my therapy sessions with Dad. I could tell she was uncomfortable by the way she changed radio stations in the car on the way to and from Dee's office. I didn't know what I could do to make her feel better. At the same time, I wanted her to suffer a little bit because I had suffered so much. And part of it was her fault.

***

The following week, Dad picked me up and took me to Dee's office. We made small talk on the way there, and Dad let me pick the music we listened to. It had been a long time since I'd been in his car, and it felt strange at first.

Dee greeted us with her usual smile. "How's it going?" she asked after we were comfortable.

I shrugged. "OK."

After what happened during our session the week before, I felt uncomfortable. I wasn't sure what Dad expected to happen this week. I think Dee knew how I felt because she didn't ask any tough questions. Instead, she asked me about school and my friends. Then we spent some time talking about movies and food.

"How would you two feel about seeing each other outside my office?" she asked.

I shrugged and looked at my dad. He was looking at me.

"Well, I'd certainly like that," he said. "But only if Gina would be OK with it. Maybe we could have dinner next weekend. Danny will be with me, so how about the three of us?"

I thought about it. It would give me something to do while Mom was out with Ben. I nodded.

"OK," I told him. "I can do that."

Dad sat back and smiled. "Great!"

"Good," Dee said. "I think you should begin seeing more of each other. Increased activities will play a big part in getting your relationship back on track. Gina, do you have any concerns about that?"

"Umm ..." I thought. "I don't think so ... I guess my mom will be OK with it."

"You should certainly clear it with your mom first," Dee advised. "I know this is something that can be difficult for kids with divorced parents. You still have two parents and both of them have authority. Since this activity will affect everyone, you'll need to make sure the scheduling works with both your mom and your dad."

"That's actually something your mom and I are talking about in our coaching sessions," Dad told me. "We're working out ways that we can communicate better without putting you in the middle. You can go ahead and tell your mom that we talked about dinner this weekend, and I will email her later to work out the details. How does that sound?"

I felt relieved. "Good," I nodded. I was glad that I wouldn't have to talk through the scheduling with my mom.

***

On the drive home, Dad asked me how I felt about everything.

"OK," I said cautiously. I wasn't sure what he wanted to hear.

"That's a relief," Dad said. "I was nervous about this process. Your mom told me that you had reservations about therapy, and I was afraid it would be difficult for you."

"No," I shook my head. "It's not difficult. Dee is really easy to talk to. I don't even think about it like therapy anymore."

"Good," Dad smiled. "I don't think of it as therapy either. I just consider it to be our talk time."

I chuckled. "That's alliteration," I told him.

"Whoa!" Dad wrinkled his face as he came to a stop at a red light. "Does your mother approve of you talking like that?"

"No, Dad." I laughed harder. "I learned it in English class. It means the words start with the same letter."

"Oh ... In that case, then, I guess it's OK," Dad looked over and winked at me. I could tell he was just pretending he didn't know the word.

"Are there any further vocabulary updates I should be aware of?" he wanted to know.

"Hmm ... How about taciturn?" I asked.

"An adjective which does not describe my daughter!" He glanced over at me.

I blushed and looked down at my lap. An awkward silence set in.

"Well ... at least, not the daughter I used to know," he said with a nudge in my direction.

I gave him a half-smile and said nothing. We were both quiet until we reached my house.

"I'm sorry about the weirdness," Dad apologized.

"It's OK," I told him. "It wasn't your fault."

"I'll see you this weekend?"

"Yeah. Umm ... you're gonna work out the timing with Mom?"

"You bet. Just let her know we talked about it, OK?"

"Yup. I'll see you then!"

***

On Saturday night, Mom left at five o'clock to meet Ben for dinner.

"Have fun with your dad," she said on her way out. "And stay out as late as you want, OK? Just let me know when to expect you back. I'll probably be home before ten." Mom sounded genuinely happy, which I attributed to her upcoming date.

"OK, I'll text you," I told her. "Have fun with Ben!"

Mom flashed me a wide smile as she grabbed her purse. "I will!" she said, and turned toward the door.

An hour later, I was sitting in the living room when I heard Dad pull up and beep. I grabbed my coat and turned off the lights. I was excited about my night out, and I was glad Mom wasn't there to watch me leave. I was still afraid of hurting her feelings.

I opened the door and slid into the front seat of Dad's car.

"Hi," I said to Dad and Danny.

"Hi, Gina," Danny said from the back seat. He was playing with some little plastic toys.

"We can't decide on where to eat," Dad told me. "Danny wants pizza, and I was thinking we should get some burritos. What do you think?"

"Hmmm ..." I thought out loud. "Pizza is overdone. Let's do burritos!"

"Aw, man," Danny moaned.

"You can pick where we go for dessert," Dad told him.

Quickly, Danny changed his tone. "Alllll rriiiiiiight!" he exclaimed. "Ice cream! Ice cream! Ice cream!"

Dad laughed, then asked me, "How was your day?"

"Fine," I told him. "I slept late, and then I read a book in the bathtub. After that, I did my nails. See?" I held up my hands to show him the stripes I painted.

"Wow, that's some impressive artwork!"

"Thanks," I said.

I was surprised at how easily I slipped into a comfortable place with Dad and Danny. There were moments when it felt like old times: the three of us hanging out while Mom was shopping or working late. We ate our burritos and then folded our tin foil to make various shapes. Danny crumpled his up and called it a baseball. Dad made an elaborate bird. I tried to make a flower but couldn't get it quite right. Finally I crumpled mine too.

"It's trash!" I said with a laugh.

"Ice cream time! Ice cream time!" Danny chanted.

I rolled my eyes. "Aw, aren't you full?"

"Not for ice cream." Danny stood up and patted his stomach.

I sighed and picked up my coat. "Oh, OK ... I guess I can make room."

Dad drove us to a specialty ice cream shop in the next town. It was a long drive, so my dinner had time to settle. By the time we arrived, I was ready for dessert. Dad ordered a sundae with three different kinds of chocolate sauce. Danny and I each got a dish of vanilla with crushed cookies.

We sat at a small round table and chatted while we ate. After we finished eating, we talked some more. Dad and Danny told me about some of their favorite things to do on their weekends together. I told them about school and some of the books I'd been reading. We even talked about Ben.

"I'm really glad your mom has a friend," Dad told us.

"What kind of friend?" Danny asked.

"A friend that she can go do things with ... like, have dinner and go to the movies."

"Are you sure?" I asked Dad.

He laughed. "Yes. I am certain. And I hope that when you meet him, you like him almost as much as your mother does."

"What about you?" I wanted to know.

"What about me? I think he's a nice guy. And, I'm still your dad. Nothing will change that."

"Well, yeah ... but ... I don't know. It's weird, I guess."

"It's only as weird as you make it," Dad told me. "You can change a situation by changing the way you look at it, you know. If you think it's weird, it is. On the other hand, you can think it's great that your mom is happy and you have another person to play board games with."

"He likes board games?" Danny was getting excited.

"I'm not sure," Dad explained. "That was just an example. The point is that your mom is a smart woman, and I don't think she'd pick a friend who wouldn't get along with you guys."

"OK," I said. "Thanks, Dad."

"You're welcome," he said with a wink.

Chapter 11: April

One night, during dinner, Mom made an announcement.

"I made some plans for us this weekend," Mom began.

Danny's face lifted. "Are we going to the zoo?" he asked.

Mom laughed and shook her head. "No, nothing quite so fun," she admitted. Then she took a deep breath. "Actually, I've made plans for us to have dinner with my friend Ben on Saturday night."

I was pleasantly surprised. "Really?" I asked. "Is it serious enough?"

Mom nodded at me in a dismissive manner and turned to Danny. "I think you'll like Ben," she told him. "You both like remote-control cars."

"All right!" Danny cheered. "Does he like board games too?"

Mom looked confused for a moment. "Um, yeah, actually he does."

Danny smiled at me, and I smiled back.

"So, what's the plan?" I asked. I was happy that I'd finally meet Ben, but at the same time I was starting to feel nervous too. I wanted to know exactly what to expect.

"Well, we're going to meet for dinner at six o'clock," Mom told me. "I'm not sure yet where dinner will be. Ben offered to cook and have us over to his house, but I told him I wasn't sure how you'd feel about that."

"If we go to his house, can I play with his cars?" Danny wanted to know.

"Perhaps," Mom told him. "But that's not really what this is about. I want to make sure you'll both be comfortable before I take you there. I don't want you to feel out of place."

"What does his daughter think?" I asked.

"Cassie won't be there," Mom said. "We decided to meet the kids separately before we all meet each other. I thought it would be a little less overwhelming for you that way. You'd only have to meet one person at a time."

"I don't care if we go to his house," I shrugged. "It would be less formal, right?"

"That's true," Mom said hesitantly. "I'll tell him that's OK ... as long as you're both sure. And I want you to know that my standards for your behavior will be no different just because we aren't in a public place."

I knew what Mom meant. She thought that Danny and I might not like Ben, and we might cause a scene. I was guessing that Dad didn't tell her about the conversation we had.

"It's OK, Mom," I told her. "You don't have to worry about us."

***

Saturday morning I woke up with a knot in my stomach. The first thing I thought of was our dinner at

Ben's house that night. I think I'd been dreaming about it too, but I didn't remember. I didn't want to go downstairs and tell my mom how I felt. I decided to call Jenny and ask for her advice.

"Hey, what's up?" she asked.

"I'm nervous," I told her. "Tonight is the night that we're meeting Ben, and my stomach feels funny. I'm afraid to eat."

"Oh, geez," Jenny sighed. "It's not a big deal. You'll meet him, and you'll eat, and you'll talk, and that will be it."

"I know," I said. "It's just that ... I don't know."

"It's just that you're nervous because it's your first time?" she laughed. "Get used to it. It won't be your last."

"Ugh. I'm so new at this!"

"I know. But don't worry. Just wear something nice. Make sure you look mature and use good manners. Don't cause a scene and don't say or do anything to embarrass your mom or you'll never hear the end of it."

"What if I don't like him?" I asked.

Jenny laughed again. "Then come home and call me, and we'll talk. Don't tell your mom, OK?"

"Seriously?"

"Yup. Sometimes it takes a while to get used to people. And your mom really likes him, so you don't want to upset her. But don't worry about that because from what you've told me, Ben is a decent guy. And your dad approves of him, so that's terrific. I don't think you have anything to worry about, but I'll keep my phone in my pocket all day and night, if you need me."

"OK," I said.

"I'm really happy for you, you know," Jenny told me.

"What do you mean?"

"Well, I think you're finally becoming like the rest of us."

"Huh?"

"You're getting to be a regular divorced kid. Like ... you're seeing both of your parents on a schedule, and your mom is dating. It looks like your life is becoming more normal."

"You mean, my life is becoming more like yours?" I asked.

"Yeah, that too. I'm just glad to see that you aren't freaking out all the time anymore. Now you can go with the flow."

"Umm ... OK."

"Give it some more time. You'll see what I mean."

I wasn't sure I knew exactly what Jenny was saying, but I got her point. I noticed the change in myself too. I was feeling more comfortable with the way things were. I was adjusting to the changes that happened in my life. And, for the most part, I felt good about it.

I went downstairs to see what my mom and Danny were up to.

"Good morning," Mom said when I walked into the kitchen. "Did you sleep OK?"

"Yeah," I said as I put a kettle of water on the stove. "Why?"

"Just wondering," Mom took a sip of her coffee. "I was a little restless. Just nerves, I guess. Are you nervous?"

"A little," I confessed. "But I think it will be OK."

Mom smiled. "I'm really nervous about meeting Cassie next week. I hope she has a similar outlook to yours."

"Oh, that's right," I said, remembering that tonight's meeting was only the first of two introductions. "Are we going to meet Cassie in two weeks?"

"Yes," Mom nodded. "That's what we were thinking. Hopefully by that time, everyone will be ready for the next phase of introductions."

I looked around and wondered if we would be hosting the next phase of introductions. Our house was small. I wasn't sure we'd all fit comfortably around the table in the kitchen. I started to wonder if Mom and Ben would get married and buy a bigger house, and then we'd have to move again and maybe Cassie and I would have to share a room ... But then I caught myself and took a deep breath. I sat down at the table with my cup of tea and remembered to take things one step at a time.

"So, what should I wear tonight?" I asked Mom.

***

We arrived at Ben's house a few minutes before we were supposed to. He greeted us at the door and kissed Mom on the cheek. Then he turned to me.

"Hi, I'm Ben," he said as he extended his hand.

"I'm Gina," I told him.

"Hi, I'm Ben," he said, turning to Danny.

Danny held out his left hand and looked confused when their palms didn't meet.

"Try your other hand," Ben suggested.

That worked. "Thanks," Danny smiled. "I'm Danny."

"The right hand works every time," Ben whispered as he winked at Danny.

I felt a pang of guilt at that moment. I felt like my dad should've been the one to teach Danny to shake hands. I took another breath and reminded myself that Ben couldn't have planned that lesson, and he wasn't trying to replace my dad.

We followed Ben to his family room, which was beside the kitchen. It was decorated with dark colors, and there were lots of books on shelves around the room. We sat down on the couch in front of a big coffee table.

"Help yourself, please," Ben gestured toward the cheese and crackers on the table.

"Would you like some help in the kitchen?" Mom asked.

"No, not at all!" Ben waved her toward the couch. "Sit. Sit and relax. Can I bring you anything?"

We all shook our heads. Mom sat on the couch with us.

"Well," she said, reaching for our hands. "Here we are. Are you feeling OK?"

Danny and I nodded. I could tell by her sweaty palm that Mom was the most nervous person in the house.

***

Mom and Ben led most of the conversation while we ate. They asked a lot of questions, hoping to generate discussion. Danny and I gave short answers, and the result was a very awkward dinner. About halfway through the meal, we settled into silence.

"You know," Ben said as we were finishing, "I'd just like to say that I am incredibly grateful that you two came over here tonight to sample my cooking. So, thank you. Thank you for coming, and thank you for eating. It has made my evening. I can't tell you how terribly nervous I was all day."

I giggled a little. "This was great, Ben," I told him. "Thanks."

"Can I interest anyone in dessert?" Ben asked, standing up. "I must confess, I did not make anything to serve you. However, I have a variety of options to offer, thanks to my grocer's freezer."

Mom and I each chose a slice of cheesecake. Danny and Ben settled on strawberry shortcake. While we ate, we talked a little more easily.

"Where did you get that?" Danny asked, pointing to a large vase in the corner that was filled with different-colored glass.

"At the beach," Ben said. "I collected that sea glass over several years. Then last year, I bought that vase to put it in. My daughter picked it out."

"Do you go to the beach a lot?" I asked.

Ben nodded, "Well, I guess that depends on what you'd call a lot. I go at least once a year. Cassie would rather we move there, but that's just not practical at this time."

"Do you go to the same place every time?"

"We go to the same area," Ben told me. "But we rent a different house each year. I enjoy seeing the same thing from different perspectives."

"Can we come to the beach with you this year?" Danny asked.

I threw an elbow at him. "That's rude," I hissed.

Mom laughed a little. "Honey, it's not appropriate to invite yourself like that," she told my brother.

Ben laughed as well. "I'd certainly consider it," he began. "But I think we should get to know each other a little more. Don't you think?"

Danny nodded excitedly. "Do you like to play board games?" he asked.

"Sure." Ben began reaching for our empty plates. "I was just going to ask if we should start a game."

"Yay!" Danny cheered.

Things were beginning to look a little better.

***

The next day Mom's phone rang. At first I couldn't tell who she was talking to. It was someone asking about our dinner the night before.

"It was fine," she said. "The kids were great."

"Yeah, they did. It was a little quiet at first, but it turned out OK."

"Not that I could tell. We didn't discuss anything beyond general small-talk-type stuff."

"Yeah, she was. She's right here. Do you want to talk to her?"

Mom handed me the phone. "It's your dad."

I was surprised. Mom must've seen it on my face because she smiled and said, "It's OK."

I took the phone. "Hi, Dad."

"Hey, Honey. I was just calling to see how everything went last night. Your mom said it went well."

"Mm hmm. Ben seems nice."

"Good. I thought so too when I met him. What are you up to today?"

"We were just talking about going for a picnic and maybe a hike."

"That sounds terrific. I won't keep you, then. Have a good time, and I'll see you this week."

"OK, thanks. Bye."

I felt better knowing that my dad was supportive of my mom's new relationship. And I was relieved to know that I could talk to him about it. I was also a little surprised at how well my parents were getting along.

**

Two weeks later I met Cassie. Our parents decided we should all go to a place where you can paint ceramics and that would give us something to do while we got to know each other. I liked the idea. I'd been painting ceramics in art class at school, and I was getting pretty good at it.

Ben and Cassie were waiting outside when we got there. Ben shook Danny's hand and Danny offered his right hand immediately. After the introductions, we headed inside and sat at a table.

Cassie and I both chose to paint rabbits. We laughed when we saw each other's selection.

"I love bunnies," she told me.

"Me too," I said. "I want one for a pet."

"My cousin has one!" Cassie said excitedly. "His name is Mister Wiggles, and he's trained to use a litterbox."

"Aww, that's so cool!"

"It is," she told me. "But he chews electrical wires, so they have to be really careful. One time he chewed through the cord to my cousin's radio, and she didn't know. When she plugged it in, the lights went out and sparks flew everywhere."

"Uh oh!"

"Yeah, they were lucky Mister Wiggles didn't chew the cord while it was plugged in."

Cassie was nice. She talked a lot about her mom and her mom's family. Ben didn't seem to mind, and sometimes he joined the discussion. I was surprised at how easy it was for her to talk about her family. I was surprised at how easy it was for her to talk to us. I still felt funny about the whole thing. I still felt a little guilty for moving on without my dad.

On our way home, Mom asked us what we thought.

"I thought it went OK," I told her.

"Mom?" Danny asked. "Are you and Ben going to get married?"

"Honey, I think it's a little too soon to think about that," Mom laughed.

"But then what is going to happen?" Danny wanted to know. "When are we going to see them again? Are they going to come live with us?"

I laughed too, but I knew how Danny felt because I felt the same way. I was reeling from the uncertainty of the situation. It felt like a lot of things were changing fast. First Mom and Dad split up, then we had to move, and now Mom was seeing someone and that could change everything all over again. I wanted someone to tell me what I could expect.

Mom slowed down and turned into a parking lot to our right. She pulled into a spot, unsnapped her seat belt and turned to face Danny.

"I love you," she told him and he smiled. She turned back to look at me. "And I love you too," she said to me.

"Thanks," I told her. "I love you too."

"Now, I'm going to be honest with both of you. I don't know what is going to happen. I can't tell you if me and Ben will ever live together or get married. I'm not sure how often we will see him and Cassie. I think a lot of it will depend on both of you and how comfortable you feel. And Cassie too. I know this is a big change for all of us, so if either of you want to talk about it, I want you to tell me how you're feeling, OK?"

Danny and I both nodded.

Mom sighed. "We just need to take things one step at a time."

Chapter 12: May

"I think you've made a ton of progress!" Dee congratulated me and my dad at our last scheduled therapy session with her.

"I can't thank you enough for your help," Dad told her. "I ... I have my daughter back."

My eyes started to tear up, and I wiped my face with the tips of my fingers.

"The happy tears are nice, aren't they?" Dee asked me.

I nodded.

Dad and I had worked through a lot in therapy. We'd talked about everything from my parents fighting, through the separation, and all the way into the possibilities of the future. During the process, Dad and I did a lot of crying. I felt like most of the time Dee spent with me, I was in tears. We learned a lot about the mistakes we'd made and promised each other we wouldn't make them again.

Dee told us to call her if we needed any more help and reminded us that she was available for individual sessions as well. We thanked her again and headed out into the evening sunshine.

"So ... ice cream?" Dad asked me. "I think we should celebrate."

"Do you think we eat too much ice cream?" I asked, laughing.

Dad raised his eyebrows at me.

"Never mind," I told him. "We should celebrate. With ice cream."

"That's the spirit!"

Dad and I got in the car, and he started the engine. He let me pull the gear shifter back until the big D turned orange. "D is for drive," he reminded me.

"Among other words," I said, thinking about the divorce.

"Are you feeling OK with all these changes?" Dad asked.

I smiled. "I am, actually. I think things are becoming normal again ... sort of."

"Well, I'm glad to hear that," Dad said slowly. "Because I've been thinking about buying a house, and I'm going to need some help picking the right one."

"You're going to move?" I asked.

"Not far," Dad said. "I want to stay in the area. I also want a pet ... and I can't decide between a kitten, a puppy or a bunny."

"Oooh, really?" I squealed.

"Sure," Dad began. "You know, D is also for dream, desire, determination ... and *dalmation*."

I smiled. "Yeah, you're right."

The thought of another new house and a pet was exciting. I felt like a new chapter of my life was beginning, and this one was looking much brighter than the previous one.

"So, what do you think?" Dad wanted to know. "Are you available to advise me on the best decisions for my family?"

"I'm your girl," I told him.

"Yes, you are," Dad said. "And I am one lucky father."

I felt the tears again. In a flash, I recalled everything Dad and I had been through together. I remembered the horrible things I'd said and done. I realized that if one of my friends had done them to me, I wouldn't be her friend anymore. And then I felt a rush of gratitude for having a father who loved me enough to stick around.

"No," I told him. "I'm the lucky one."

About the Author

Tara Eisenhard is an ex-wife and the child of cooperatively divorced parents. From these life experiences came her belief that families can evolve, not dissolve, through the process. She has studied divorce and blended-family dynamics and is passionate about sharing her knowledge with others. Tara lives in Central Pennsylvania.

CPSIA information can be obtained at www.ICGtesting.com
Printed in the USA
LVOW08s1801161013

357230LV00001B/203/P